ERICA KUDISCH

DON'T FEED THE TROLLS

RIPTIDE
PUBLISHING

Riptide Publishing
PO Box 1537
Burnsville, NC 28714
www.riptidepublishing.com

Don't Feed the Trolls
Copyright © 2017 by Erica Kudisch

Cover art: L.C. Chase, lcchase.com/design.htm
Editor: Carole-ann Galloway
Layout: L.C. Chase, lcchase.com/design.htm

From "For Good," from the Broadway musical *Wicked*
Music and Lyrics by Stephen Schwartz
Copyright © 2003 Stephen Schwartz.
All rights reserved. Used by permission of Grey Dog Music (ASCAP).

ISBN: 978-1-62649-559-3

First edition
April, 2017

Also available in ebook:
ISBN: 978-1-62649-558-6

Kudisch, Erica

ERICA KUDISCH

DON'T FEED THE TROLLS

RIPTIDE
PUBLISHING

For Abbi, who fights.

TABLE OF CONTENTS

 PROLOGUE

FROM: Martin Summers (summers@summerstorm.net)
TO: Fatiguee Altestis (je.suis.fatiguee@qmail.com)
CC: Publicity (publicity@summerstorm.net), Max Long (veep1@
summerstorm.net), Luis Lender (veep2@summerstorm.net), Farah
Mackinnon (erstory@summerstorm.net), Carl Jenkins (chair@geekon.
com)

SUBJECT: Eternal Reign Novelization Contest Results

Her Grace the Duchess Fatiguee,

Congratulations! We're sending this out before the official article drops on the website, in case your spam filter eats the general notification.

A winner is you!

Not just *a* winner. *The* winner. The panel really enjoyed The Annals of Altestis *and thinks you and your knights have been taking advantage of the gameplay freedoms of* Eternal Reign *in exciting and innovative ways. GeeKon should be in touch with you in a few hours about your badge, and you can contact the publicity department (CC'd above) if you have any questions before the convention.*

We look forward to meeting with you at GeeKon to discuss future opportunities. Our creative team is always looking for new ideas, and who better than the players to shape the direction of the game? In the meantime, keep enjoying Eternal Reign.

Martin Summers

President, SummerStorm Entertainment Inc.

summers@summerstorm.net

"I have to have a creative role otherwise I simply wouldn't come into work." —Hideo Kojima

Holy shit.

This had better be real. I'm not about to go into literal shock over a hoax. But all those email addresses are real; I would know, I sent the manuscript to half of them two months ago and the other half are household names, at least in a household like mine. So it's real. Seventy percent chance of real. I can take those odds. I'm allowed to get excited about those odds. Those are callback odds.

Okay. Odds. Calculating odds by facts is better than sitting here wondering. Fact one: The email was apparently sent forty minutes ago. I received it forty seconds ago, but hey, Alain's hogging the bandwidth. Fact two: I'll have confirmation when—if—it drops on the website, and while that's not impossible to fake and there might be something lost in translation, it's damned difficult, and if someone went through the trouble to rile me up, I should probably let them. Fact three: I'm going into shock anyway, because a seventy percent chance of real apparently doesn't let me decide whether I'm excited or not, and screw the facts.

I shove back my computer chair and try not to shriek *too* loud.

Jackie bangs on the wall between our bedrooms anyway. "All right in there?"

"Fine!"

"I thought it wasn't a raid night," Alain calls from the living room. I didn't have my door closed, so now that I've rolled the chair back I can see him sprawled on the couch, simultaneously playing *Ultimate Odyssey XIII* (or XIV, I've lost count) and breaking in a new pair of drag shoes. He catches my eye and shifts from obvious concern to more optimistic surprise. "Good news?"

"Maybe," I admit, and wheel the chair closer to the doorway. It doesn't fit through (we had to build it in here when I moved in) but hey, close is close. "You remember that contest thing I told you about?"

"The Kristin Chenoweth master class thing?"

"No, the *Eternal Reign* thing." And whoomp, there it is: even if I really have won this contest, I shouldn't have entered in the first place. I'm supposed to be auditioning and pressuring my agent into finding me work that isn't *Oklahoma* in Oklahoma for the third summer in a row, and here I am, playing MMOs eight hours a day and writing a hundred thousand-plus words of glorified bluebook. But never mind that, and never mind the acid guilt threatening to eat its way out of my stomach. Those hundred thousand words of roleplay logs landed me a seventy percent real chance of an industry interview.

They might seriously hire me. Or at least consult me for user-generated content. It wouldn't be acting, but it would be a job (maybe!) doing something I love and impressing myself on the media I've enjoyed for *years*. Isn't that all I really want from acting anyway? To do what I love and get recognition for it?

Since Alain can't hear inside my head (and he definitely can't hear much at all over the mediocre English voice acting in this game), he didn't get all that, and asks, "What, you're in the finals?"

"Actually, I think I won."

I swear to god, the *Ultimate Odyssey* victory theme plays. Alain puts the PS3 controller down. "You *think*?"

"I mean, I just got an email about it. From SummerStorm."

Alain stares at me like I've started speaking Chinese instead of French. Then blinks. Then drops the controller, mutters, "Thank god for autosave," and throws himself at me.

I'm sitting in the desk chair. He's bigger than me (even if he's assholishly skinny) and wearing the spikiest knockoff Louboutins I've ever seen. Somehow, Alain manages not to scratch me while he's hugging me like a big dog whose master just got home. And he's shouting congratulations to high heaven, so fast I can't make out the words. I hug him back, as best I can.

"Let me see!" Alain trills, spinning my desk chair around to get into my bedroom. "Still up?"

"Yeah. Make sure I'm not hallucinating?" Not that Alain will be able to do much more checking than I have, but—

"It's real," Jackie says from her room. "It dropped on Twitter."

I scramble for my phone, since Alain's evidently taken over my computer—and the phone isn't in my pocket. I left it on the desk. Whoops. But a couple of passwords and swipes later, it's real there too:

@EternalReign (Verified member)

ER Contest results are in. Congrats to Duchess Fatiguee of Altestis, and her counts and knights! bit.ly/gh345ny

Well, there goes seventy percent real. It's now Twitter real.

Alain pounces on me again, so hard my phone goes flying. Thankfully, it doesn't hit either of my monitors, just the wall. And yup, I'm in literal shock, because even though I'm standing now, I still feel like Alain's holding up most of my weight.

And then, no, it's not only him. Jackie's here too. Naked, because Jackie, and Naked-Jackie-Watching-Anime is a *thing*, and I've definitely interrupted it, but here she is and it's a three-way hug. Like the old days. I think all our Musketqueer tattoos are out too, poetic as it is.

Jackie, Alain, and I met about fifteen years ago, when my family came to America and I wound up at the French-American School upstate. They had the dubious honor of being the only out kids in our high school until I got there. Alain thereafter encouraged Jackie to hit on me, *"because as long as there's another girl who likes girls they might as well be together,"* he said then, in his inestimable fourteen-year-old wisdom. Little did he know we wouldn't hook up, just team up, and then it was all for one and one for all. Matching tattoos the summer we all graduated: three sabers raised high. And then Jackie, who still hasn't outgrown her habit of taking in prodigals and strays, got the gang together again after college to pay less rent than we should on an apartment in Manhattan. I swear, it started as me needing a place to crash when I wasn't on tour, but hey, I haven't *been* on tour in three years, and—

God. Can't I fucking be happy about anything?

"So what's next?" Alain asks, and a good thing too, otherwise it's maudlin o'clock. "Prizes? Interviews?"

"Both. I'm supposed to get a free badge to GeeKon, and then interview there."

"Where's GeeKon?"

Jackie answers before I can: "Seattle, usually November."

Of course she knows. Jackie's been to more conventions than me and Alain combined, since she does panels as Lady Francois, fanfiction author and smut peddler extraordinaire. As double lives go, hers might be the least embarrassing of all of ours. She writes millions of words about magical girls in love and saves teenagers from a life bereft of female sexuality. Alain performs in drag clubs around the city as Ivy LeVine—well, that's not embarrassing, just hard to talk about with new people. Not that there are many new people, since Alain meets far more new people as Ivy than he does as himself.

And I, um. When I'm not Daphne Benoit, perpetually struggling actress, I'm the Duchess Fatiguee of Altestis, in the fictional world of *Eternal Reign*. Also known as Daphne Benoit, MMORPG addict.

Hi.

"Dinner's on me," Jackie says, disengaging from the hug pile to head to her room and get her phone. And possibly underwear.

I swear it's reflexive. "You don't have to—"

"Let her," Alain says. He bounds back to the couch (bounding in seven-inch pumps is a feat known only to epic-level drag queens) and picks up the PS3 controller again. "If she doesn't, Orin will. And if Orin doesn't call within five minutes, I'll buy the beer myself."

I sit down on the armchair, since Alain takes up pretty much the entire couch with his legs stretched out like this. I don't know how he plays sitting less than bullet-straight with his feet on the floor. Then again, Alain doesn't do *anything* bullet-straight. "I'm not taking that bet."

Alain grins. "You won't have to. Your phone's ringing."

No, it's not, that's a text tone. Same difference, though. And once I read it, I'm glad I have the prudence not to make bets about Orin.

Provisions en route, Your Grace. The magic of Seamless conveys gifts of pizza and beer from far-off Rochester. Celebrate as befits a benevolent despot! (Also congrats, you.)

God, Orin's a dork. But a dork that's mostly made me smile for, what now, eight years? Fuck I'm old. Well, we're all old. And fed, apparently. I text back, *Your tithe is accepted, my loyal Sachem.* And then, for good measure, so he doesn't get the wrong idea, *(Thanks! Couldn't have done it without you.)* Which may not be quite enough to dissuade him from the wrong idea. But it's too late now, and I should warn Jackie not to order too much food.

I take care of all that—can't stop Jackie from ordering entirely, but she can afford it and leftovers aren't a crime. And then there's nothing to do but wait, and celebrate a little.

I head back into my room, sit down at the computer. It's real. I'm really going to meet with the creators of *Eternal Reign*. I really impressed someone, won something, for the first time in ages. I can relax. I can gloat. I can scroll through the announcement websites and tweets and maybe even post it on Facebook for all my people who don't want to read it in English. I tilt back the chair until it creaks, just breathe for a while.

Something good. Finally, something real is also something good.

I should log in and announce it to my knights. It's their story too, after all. I boot up *Eternal Reign*, skip the auto-updates and head straight for the messaging system. I last logged on about three hours ago and it's not a campaign night, so most of these new messages are probably about the contest. Good to see the knights are in line—

—or not.

GONNA FUCK YOUR FACE BITCH WRITE ABOUT THAT
go home u fake cunt
gtfo feminazi scum
How about you put my dick in your fucking Anals of Allthesetits?
looks like someone got a facial from Summers!!
Congratulations, whore. Gonna show my appreciation for your fucking trash romance novel by pillaging your ass, just like you want it.
kill yourself
WRITE ABOUT ME CLIMBING IN YOUR WINDOW AND RAPING YOU TO DEATH BITCH

. . . Holy shit.

CHAPTER ONE

There is unrest in the Duchy of Altestis. It's not just that the borders are under siege—they are always under siege, since the *eternal* part of *Eternal Reign* is a misnomer—nor that there seems to be similar unrest in her neighboring provinces, even though that's entirely true. No, the unrest in Altestis is the legend of the Fisher King in action.

Every day for the last several weeks when the Duchess Fatiguee first logs in, she deals with her correspondence. She receives dozens, sometimes hundreds, of missives each morning. Some of these are petitions from her landholders and knights for assistance or repair. Some are information about server downtime or upgrades. A few are congratulations, especially from the players whose stories she included in her annals, which have since been recognized by the Council of Gerents. But the vast majority of the missives are requests that she, alternately, get raped or die. Sometimes simultaneously. Sometimes not in that order.

(That most of these requests are directed at me instead of Fatiguee is largely inconsequential. But she's made of code, and I'm not, and the developers didn't write rape into the pillaging mechanic. Small mercies, I guess.)

It's been a week. The save file of harassment screencaps is bigger than the final draft of the *Annals*, because I'm saving the images as hi-res as I can so no one can say I'm faking them. Well, so fewer people can say I'm faking them. They can say whatever they want, apparently. Free country, free server. Free-to-play game. Free speech according to the populist definition. I've spent more time on the phone with the predictably imbecilic NYPD than I have on campaign, and that's basically what they said. Talking smack isn't illegal in America.

It wouldn't matter back in France either. Madame Guillotine didn't talk smack. She just lopped off heads.

According to a lot of semi-legit internet lawyers, if I want the cops to do anything about it, I have to document everything. No one ever tells you that documenting everything means reading it all twice.

Of course I know that gaming while female is some kind of sin to these assclowns, but they don't know that Fatiguee has a female player and they're *still* going on about bitch, whore, cunt. They assume I've got one of those, and I do, but even if I didn't they'd say I did. Because apparently it's an affront to look female whether you are or not, to have any ostensibly female parts or traits or whatever for someone with a dick to exploit and correct.

God, what a fine fucking line to walk. Here I am, assuming these dickheads have dicks.

It's playground bullshit all over again, Not All Men and Yes All Women, like woman is some monolithic universal concept. I'm playing a game on the internet and these trolls literally can't see what I am on the other side, and yet they assume enough to feminize it. Nuance doesn't exist on the internet. It barely exists in the real world. Hell, the drag queen I live with insists on being one or the other and nothing between, and clearly he's got more right to angst about gender than I do.

I should probably do something else. I don't know, work. Go to a dance class. Stage combat. Redo my audition binder. Something that gets me out of the apartment. But anything that would get me out of the house either costs money or nets nothing.

I could clean the place. I owe Alain and Jackie anyway. Of course I told them right away, if by *told them* I mean *flipped the fuck out immediately* and thereupon converted the celebratory dinner into a pity party. I then proceeded to get blackout drunk, which was a great idea at the time but horrible in the morning since I concluded, upon waking up, that the whole thing was a nightmare and subsequently there was no reason for me not to log on. Which meant lather, rinse, repeat.

Right. Cleaning the apartment. At least that gets me away from the computer.

I throw on the crappiest shirt I have—*How I Mine For Fish?*, circa 2005—and get to work. My room isn't that bad, just a couple of shirts that missed the hamper and a rug that needs shaking. I'll find more to do in the living room, I think—yup, Alain left it a mess. He doesn't mind me sorting his makeup, so I get to work on the table and organize it all back into his kit. God, it's nice not thinking about anything but whether honey is supposed to be lighter or darker than mahogany. Once that's done, I get out the Swiffer and go to town.

For a couple of years, right after college, I was a literal French maid. I couldn't get any work temping no matter how I tried to hide my accent. If I had a dollar for every time someone made a joke about putting me in the proper uniform, I'd have more dollars than I made. But the skills stick with you, even if you started out a rich brat whose parents are still appalled that you're not behind a desk at the UN. Fuck, I'll never be able to tell them about this online ridiculousness— Nope. Cleaning! Not thinking! Scrubbing floors and washing walls and emptying chamber pots!

Better. Menial. But better.

In fact, I should put on some music that has nothing to do with gaming and everything to do with my ostensible choice of career. I turn on the *Cabaret* revival soundtrack (because whatever else is going on, my life sucks less than interwar Germany) and knuckle down in the living room. Act one passes in a perpetuity of Lysol, and by the time I'm running out of things to do, "Two Ladies" is playing.

Well, that's just prophetic.

The last time I was in *Cabaret* was summer stock in Nebraska, five years ago maybe. The guy playing the Emcee was a grade-A asshole, but I still wanted to be in "Two Ladies" because that song is hilarious and one of the only ways to feature in that ensemble that doesn't involve a gorilla suit. But ironically enough, the staging for "Two Ladies" only requires one, because in the international language of theater the gag of a man crossdressing is funnier than a woman attempting comedy, and ever since the movie version staged it that way the song has been *about* bisexuality. Therefore, with only one slot for a woman available and all six of us in the ensemble gunning for it, of course I didn't get the part.

They picked the most feminine girl. And the butchest chorus boy. Because they wanted the audience to be a hundred percent aware that one of those girls has a dick. Because that's funny.

You know what else is funny? My agent's special ringtone. It's "All I Care About Is Love" from *Chicago*, and it's playing right now, and despite the shows having the same composers, it completely clashes with my *Cabaret* playlist.

I answer the phone, *then* turn the music off, *then* speak. "*Bonjour*, Julio."

"English, Daphne," he chides.

I should smile. Fake it till you make it, and all that. So I fake it. "I assume you're calling with good news?"

"Unfortunately no, but I'll give you the good parts first. You've got a guaranteed slot at next season's *Live From Lincoln Center* auditions. They like you, they just don't have a place for you this year."

Great. Just great. "Or last year. I think they've been saying that since Tiler Peck sniped me in *Carousel*."

Julio evidently takes this as a joke. Maybe he can hear the fake smile. "Well, they wanted someone who looks more like a ballerina, that's all. And I think they've got the same excuse this time. Wait a second, I've got their notes right here."

"Fine." It's not going to do anything for the shreds of my self-esteem, but a good actor always takes the note. Let the authorities say What They See, tailor yourself to it.

"All right, here we are. 'Excellent dancer, incongruent with rest of ensemble.' See? Not bad at all. They just wanted a uniform chorus line."

"Okay. Incongruent *how*, Julio?"

"They didn't exactly write that in the email. But if I had to guess based on the ones I know got in, it's probably your arms."

"My arms."

"Yeah, I'd say they wanted delicate arms. You look like you work out, you know that, and your tattoo probably drew their eye. It's not the most feminine art in the world. Maybe cover it up next time and see if that works."

It's his job to say this. It's my job to hear it and accept it and move on. And it's better than the whole world of crap on the internet I'm not permitting myself to think about. Marginally.

No, it's not even marginally better: it's exactly the same. It's still a man, telling me to be a woman, because anything else is aberrant.

"Note taken," I tell him. It's a bald-faced lie, of course, but I'm an actress after all. And once we've taken care of the rest of this business, I head back to my room and stuff a bandana into my kit bag. For next time.

Alain walks in when I've already started on the kitchen, so I must have successfully not thought about things for half an hour. "Hey," he says. "One of those days?"

"I sorted your box," I nonanswer. "How was work?"

He plunks a small Sephora bag down on the coffee table, right next to the makeup I've already dealt with. I can tell he wants to talk about it—the raised eyebrow is definitely not penciled in. But he doesn't speak up. Alain knows when to fold 'em. Words, I mean. Not clothes. "Not bad. Definitely going to see the same bachelorettes at Red Stamp tonight. I hope they tip better when I'm wearing the face instead of putting it on them."

Good, he's distracted enough to talk about himself. I keep unpacking the dry-goods cabinet. "They probably will."

"Yeah, unless they pass out." He checks that the countertop is clean before he swings up and sits on it. "What do you think Ivy should wear tonight?"

"What are you performing?"

"I don't know, it's fishbowl night."

The last time I saw Alain—as Ivy—at a fishbowl night, he drew "All About That Bass." It didn't exactly work, since he barely even pads back there. "In that case, I don't know either. Got anything new?"

He grins. "Thought you'd never ask." He lifts one wrist and waggles his fingers, flashing the spiky cuff and stacked silver claw rings. "Think I can build something around these?"

By Alain's own condemnation, I have about as much style as a toilet paper shoe trail. But the answer to that question is always "Yeah." It looks enough like what Alain usually wears—he tends to mirror the Japanese RPG heroes he loves so much, even if the trademarked Nomura looks aren't designed with Algerians like him in mind—belts and all his jewelry stacked on the left like armor. Ivy doesn't look like she walked out of Ultimate Odyssey, more like she walked out of Rammstein's apartment at four in the morning to get another box of condoms and some coke. I'm not sure claw rings are quite right for Ivy, but there's enough of a difference between the two styles that maybe I'm just not seeing something. And Alain's the kind of person who cares about both of those styles as belonging to separate people. Alain is Alain, and Ivy is Ivy.

It must be really useful having someone else to retreat to.

Wait. *Wait.*

It's not unheard of. I've never done it, just because I've wanted to see more women in the games I play, but I know a few guys in my fief who play female knights, and a count with a female player. But it's impossible to know for some of the others. Not everyone uses voice chat, and even if they did, it's not as if voices in the middle range can be identified as one or the other. If my inbox full of bullshit is anything to go on, the trolls will assume male avatars have male players. And I've never taken it at anything but face value: if a player tells me he's a guy, he's a guy.

Other players might do that for me. On a new server. In a new fief. And no one would be the wiser.

More importantly, no one would be threatening to rape me to death. Probably.

"Earth to Daphne, come in Daphne," Alain says, leaning in and twirling his finger in my face.

I drop the sponge. Not on his leggings, but close enough. "Sorry. Just trying to fix my life."

He clunks his head against mine, nose to nose. "You know we've got you, right? One for all."

"All for one," I countersign. "I know." And I do believe him, but I can handle this alone. I think.

I boot up character creation, crack my neck, and go to work.

Eternal Reign runs on the premise that back in the Age of Discovery, Magellan sailed off the end of the Earth and wound up in the endless oceans of another world. Five races compete for turf and resources, Tudor-style: Settlers, Kharthi, Aqueian, Touched, and Liqing. Fatiguee is Touched: I set her up to play a long courtiering game since I was going to be dealing with real-world shows and schedules, and it's pretty easy to form alliances among other Touched. I could make this alt another, but that kind of defeats the purpose of making an alt in the first place. He's going to be different.

And a he. Yes. I'm going to tick that box and be a guy on the internet.

Only two options in the game, after all.

And I'll play a Settler, I think. If I'm going to make a new character on a new server environment where I don't know any of the players, I should probably create something straightforward and adaptable, since I don't know the lay of the land. I don't think I'll have to go pirate, but it's a safe bet to build a decent seaman. I design a rougish-looking fellow, sun-browned, blond hair, kitted out in a leather doublet and a facial tattoo. If only it was this easy in real life, creating a face to show the world, a person to be.

Skill points in capital, craft, persuasion—no, not persuasion. I'm not going to play a court game. I know what it's like for my counts to be wrapped up in Fatiguee's. I guess that's the double-edged sword of *Eternal Reign:* with the players creating the content, I don't have to play in a game as cutthroat as the one I created. I could join a merchants' guild or a pirate flotilla or assist in the defense of a wargame, depending on the climate of the new server. Navigation, then. I'll make him a navigator. That's always useful, I remember one of Orin's knights lamenting that his expeditionary force is held up because the navigator just started law school, and they can't find a new one. If the low-level knights here have the same problem, I'll gladly step in to fill that void. So male, Settler, navigator. That fills out the rest of my skills and stats easily enough, and from there, I only need a name.

Names are always the hardest. Hell, I only came up with *Fatiguee* because I literally said I was *tired of looking* and it stuck. I start typing in random test letters, and nothing's right. Cousins' names, nope. Characters from other games, nope. I can't use my default ones if I don't want to be found out, in case the trolls decide to track me here.

I don't want even Orin to guess that I've hopped servers because I've been effectively banned from my own.

Banned. Benedict. Ban Edict. *Bannedict.* That'll work. I'd trust a player who used that name to have a sense of humor. There I go: he's Bannedict, and a few clicks later I wind up with my starting fief, Verohno.

That was easier than I thought it would be, honestly. And safer. I already feel like a weight's off my shoulders, starting from scratch. I don't have to deal with more aggro than any other new player, and even that shouldn't be much since I'm starting out in charted waters. I bring up the map screen: Verohno is right on the edge of Count Rynek's territory, so I guess he's my liege, and the sovereign is—

NEW MESSAGE: Duchess Uhruu summons you. [Text] [Voice] [Video]

Well, that was fast. As Fatiguee I usually let the counts handle new players if they're on, since they'll be likely to interact with them directly.

I click [Text]. Voice chat would be easier—but text is safer. I think.

UHRUU*D: *Welcome, traveler. New to ER?*

Uhruu's character portrait shows a Kharthi female with saturated green skin and lots of gold bling in her seaweed hair. A quick look at her stats shows I just walked into a convoy game: her fleet is sixty ships strong, but her land holdings are twenty-seven, close to the bare minimum for a duchess. That's not a bad scenario for a new navigator, and a new navigator in the hands of a veteran player like me is deceptively useful. Duchess Uhruu's been playing for at least a year, so she'd know that, but she's sent me a neutral hail. I make sure to type differently than I usually do, just in case someone traces this back to me.

BANNEDICT: *hail! no, old soul, new alt*

I'm not going to pretend otherwise. It's to her advantage anyway.

UHRUU*D*: *Great! If you're new to this server, I'm glad to lay down the rules.*

Rules? In *Eternal Reign*? Well, if she's the most powerful person on the server, she can make whatever rules she wants. But I know most of my knights and counts live by *Rien n'est vrai, tout es permis,* and relish that they're playing a game where *nothing is sacred, PVP is permitted*, and until a week ago I would have counted myself among them. But if Uhruu plans to lay down the law, unlike me with Fatiguee, that means she can effectively punish those who break it, doesn't it?

Either way, I'm curious.

UHRUU*D*: *I know it's a game, so I can't stop you from trying to infiltrate my ranks. Character-versus-character violence isn't something I can explicitly prevent, though I assure you, it's something I can avenge. But player-versus-player violence, including harassment, doxxing, and use of real-world sabotage to influence in-game events, will meet with in-game ostracism and out-of-game reporting to the Council of Gerents.*

Those are the best words I could possibly hear now, shy of *You just got cast as Hamlet in the new Broadway production* or *Every single person who spammed your account has come down with genital warts*.

BANNEDICT: *that's a relief. i came here to avoid exactly that, so i think we'll get along fine*

UHRUU*D*: *I'm sorry. I've been there. You need any help in advance, just say the word.*

BANNEDICT: *thanks*

UHRUU*D*: *No problem.*

That's the last I hear from her for a while: another hail pops up, standard LFG, and it turns out I was entirely correct to make a navigator. A small fleet under Count Rynek needs assistance on a pirate hunt, raid scheduled tomorrow at 7 p.m. EST, and yes, I'm down. Rynek imparts a good place to grind solo, just outside of charted waters, and I've got enough nav skill to tell that he's not lying, so there goes the better part of three hours.

It's strange, not having the story to tell like I have with Fatiguee, but hey, maybe Sir Bannedict will become a character in someone else's. And it's relaxing, which is more than I can say about everything I've done as Fatiguee for the last two years. High risk, high reward, I guess, until the reward starts being Grade-A Bullshit.

Or fish heads. Great, looks like I have to find someone to melt those into machine oil . . .

Six hours and two failed attempts at bomb-making later, the Duchess Uhruu's window pops up again.

UHRUU*D*: *Did you find someone to work with?*

BANNEDICT: *yeah. it's kind of you to check in*

UHRUU*D*: *You haven't played with many conscientious sovereigns, have you?*

BANNEDICT: *you have no idea*

UHRUU*D*: *Ha. Well, don't name names unless you have to worry about them here.*

BANNEDICT: *i don't think i will*

BANNEDICT: *i came from another server and i don't think they'll follow me*

BANNEDICT: *rubicon crossed, bridges burned*

BANNEDICT: *if you can burn bridges made of pixilated water i mean*

UHRUU*D*: *Haha yeah. I get it. Just message me if you have to. Or if you don't, that's fine too.*

BANNEDICT: *i will*

UHRUU*D*: *Should I let you go?*

BANNEDICT: *no, sorry*

BANNEDICT: *you're not annoying me i promise, im flattered*

BANNEDICT: *english isn't my first language and i've been told i can come across final in it*

BANNEDICT: *but i'm blunt in french too so yeah*

UHRUU*D*: *Canadian?*

BANNEDICT: *no, french living in the us*

UHRUU*D*: *Ah, cool. I ask because I'm in Seattle and we get a lot of disgruntled Vancouverites. And half of my counts are Quebecois.*

BANNEDICT: *ha*

BANNEDICT: *that's going to help on voice chat*

UHRUU*D*: *I don't doubt it. You're working your way up as a navigator?*

BANNEDICT: *yeah*

UHRUU*D*: *I'll convey it to the others. The highest ranked is Count Dhalinhwa. IRL he's got a 3 year old so he needs all the help he can get.*

BANNEDICT: *i'll keep that in mind*

BANNEDICT: *you have a tight handle on this*

UHRUU*D*: *I got sick of lawless players.*

BANNEDICT: *i don't blame you*

BANNEDICT: *it's why i'm here*

BANNEDICT: *but if you're that tired of it why keep playing here*

UHRUU*D*: *You can hate the players without hating the game, I guess. Or you can create places within the game where you don't hate the players. I know a lot of people use ER to be assholes, but it's got the potential to be so much more. And if they've got the freedom to be assholes, I've got the freedom to be decent.*

BANNEDICT: *amen*

UHRUU*D*: *So yeah. The game's what the players make it, and I'm making it the kind I want to play, because if they can, so can I.*

BANNEDICT: *i've never heard anyone put it that way before*

BANNEDICT: *is it forward to say that's really beautiful?*

UHRUU*D*: *Forward, maybe, but flattering. And thank you.*

BANNEDICT: *you're welcome*

BANNEDICT: *i hope i can do the same*

UHRUU*D*: *I know you can. And again, thank you. Sometimes I need to hear I'm not crazy.*

BANNEDICT: *well you're not*

BANNEDICT: *those guys are the crazy ones trying to scare people out of having a good time*

UHRUU*D*: *And this guy isn't?*

BANNEDICT: *no, this guy just wants to chart the endless sea without hate mail popping up every five seconds*

UHRUU*D*: *Well then this guy and I should get along just fine.*

BANNEDICT: *this guy agrees completely*

UHRUU*D*: *Haha. Does this guy have a name he'd prefer to be called OOC? Mine would be Laura.*

I type my real name reflexively, like everything else in this conversation—fuck, she's easy to talk to. And she gets the harrassment, which is more than I can say for anyone else I've talked to so far, even Alain and Jackie.

But Fatiguee's name is already out there, contest winner and all, and my real name won't be far behind. I shouldn't use it.

And Uhruu—Laura—is already thinking of me as a guy. *A name he'd prefer.* That is the whole point, isn't it? To be someone else.

At least my name has a masculine alternative.

BANNEDICT: *daphnis*

BANNEDICT: *my name is daphnis*

UHRUU*D*: *Nice to meet you, Daphnis.*

BANNEDICT: *enchante*

CHAPTER
TWO

The court game in Altestis is an elaborate intrigue going back over two years. The young Duchess Fatiguee, barely three months under her ducal coronet, had the prospect of some off-world commitments that she couldn't shake. (In fact, she was short-listed for a supporting role in a certain French-Korean collaborative film about trains and cannibalism, but the director ultimately decided that the character should be English and that Tilda Swinton looked better with false teeth. It was a near thing.) Because of this, the duchess needed to appoint a castellan to oversee her realm and her fleet, and, in order to avoid accusations of favoritism, she encouraged her counts to curry for esteem in her sight. This resulted in factions, tournaments, large-scale trade expeditions, four duels to the death, eight hookups, three breakups, and one out-of-game divorce.

Eternal Reign is Serious Business.

She has since employed an elaborate system of appointments and rotations. In game, this takes the form of her counts and countesses increasing their tithes, prospecting and conquering in her name, and systematically assassinating one another. Since *Eternal Reign* attracts a lot of Shakespeare enthusiasts and the disaffected non-Luddite fringes of the Society for Creative Anachronism, Duchess Fatiguee was placed in the role of Queen Elizabeth, which suited her player just fine. And aside from the divorce and one of the duels to the death (and one incident involving 5,000 dubloons and a real-life application of a fish to parts uncharted), a good time was had by all.

The duchess's current favorite, Count Sachem, has cycled into and out of the position about fifteen times. Orin's perfectly okay with this, as far as I know, since he's known me in meatspace for years and seems to have a handle on the IC/OOC distinction, which is more than I can say for some of the others.

But hey, lucky me! I don't have to worry about that right now, because I have an alt. Let the counts fight among themselves. Maybe they'll forget they had someone to fight over. And Orin's always wanted to hold down the fort anyway.

Orin texts, *My Lady?*

I am become Asshole, Destroyer of Worlds.

Lucky for him, well, both of us, it's not a raid night on the new server. And he doesn't know about the new server.

Again, Orin texts, *(Busy IRL? Is it the master class?)*

No, it's not the master class. It has nothing to do with my torpid acting career and everything to do with the fact that I've been ignoring my imaginary commitments in favor of other imaginary commitments.

I know we haven't spoken much this last week, he goes on without punctuation, because now it's not interrogative. Another one follows, quick as desperation, *I've bee trying to give you space*, then, immediately, *Been*, because Orin grades papers and has brought his sticklerness into the world outside of academia. I can't help smiling. *But can I call?*

Yes. If he's asking, it must be important, and I don't want him to be as put out as I am. And then I bring up my contacts and start calling him, but of course he beats me to it.

"Hey."

"Hey yourself," he says. "I know everything's not all right, but is everything else?"

Cute. I can picture him: eyebrows raised, beard a little twitchy while he tries not to smile too much. And no, everything else isn't all right, but enough is, so I can say, "Yeah. I'm managing. Are the undergrads settled yet?"

"Not for another week. So I'm okay to keep the Keep a while longer, but not that much longer."

Right. He has a real life. And a real job, as real as any job in academia anyway. All things are hypothetical until he finishes his dissertation. Actually, in a philosophy department, all things are hypothetical. *Cogito, ergo* something else. "Fine. I'll log on. Anything I should know?"

"About that." He tends to do that little anime neck-rub thing when he has to deliver bad news in a good way. I'll bet he's doing it now. This is not helping me feel like less of an asshole. "You've got about thirty new knights waiting to present themselves at court."

I must have heard wrong. "Thirteen? *Treize?*"

"No, thirty. Three tens. *Trente.*"

Even thirteen would be a lot for one week. "Someone's outsourcing."

"Yeah, I thought so too. Not at first. I mean I thought that it was because of the *Annals*. You know, the contest."

"No shit, Orin."

"Sorry."

"It's fine."

"Okay. So. You have new knights. Could be good press, could be trolls lying in wait. Both, I think. I've screened them the best I can, but I don't have your ops."

"And for that I need to log on." Well, I already said I would. "Give me a minute?"

"Of course. I'll get everyone in the hall. Muster?"

"Muster."

"I'll get on that. Two hours should do it, I think Krozin's company is finishing up a raid." And then, just before I hang up, "Are you sure you're okay?"

No, Orin. No, I'm not. And you're so perceptive about it that you can tell all the way from Rochester by my voice alone. But because of that you'll know there's nothing lost in translation when I say, "Yeah, I'll be fine," emphasis on the future tense and yet still a lie.

Wherever possible, we hold musters in character in Altestis. It's not a rule, merely custom. But with so many new knights, it's an obvious show of power when I sign in and voice-override everyone in the metaphysical vicinity.

"The duchess speaks," I say, in English, because lingua franca is frankly easier.

Fuck, do I wish I had this much authority in the real world. Nearly everyone shuts up, and the ones that don't get shushed by everyone else. It's the equivalent of walking onstage and having all eyes on me, without leaving my desk.

And it's beautifully staged in my head. Fatiguee, accoutered like a Star Trek take on the Lady of Shalott, reclines on her throne, draped as elegantly as her gown. Courtiers, mostly Touched like her but a smattering of the other races, look up from their private conversations, some intrigued, some dubious, a few with thinly veiled resentment, but every last one of them with envy. The riot of color shifts to the glow of upturned faces and the glitter of armor and jewels. They place the scene in my hands. They place themselves in my hands.

If I had the stomach for it, I'd start transcribing for the annals. Which is to say, I don't.

"I am grateful, as always, to those of you who have overseen Altestis in my absence," I begin. "It is to my understanding that some of you have taken on new vassals in the interim. Counts, in order of precedence determined by the size of your demesne as of our last muster, please present your new knights."

"The size of the *last* muster?" someone asks—Krozin, I think, and double-check. Yes, it's his feed.

"Yes. Which puts you third, I believe. Behind Count Sachem and Countess Regnava."

Krozin scoffs. "I've got twenty knights waiting."

"All the more reason for you to go later," Orin, or rather Sachem, says. "Or even last, with that many."

"She's back, Sachem, you don't get to play duke."

A few of the microphone feeds shudder, laughing. It's always a little eerie when the icons and avatars stand there with their default expressions while the players speak, but hey, a hundred thousand words of bluebooking attest that I have a good enough imagination to fill in the gaps.

I laugh as well, in character at least. "Sachem, you have a point, but so does he. My order of precedence stands."

Krozin groans. "We've been raiding for six hours already. How much more time do we have to wait?"

"Let your men take a break. If you've got twenty knights, there can't be enough ahead of you to make a difference."

"Fine," he says.

"So, Sachem. First in my heart," I add, to lighten the mood. "How many?"

"Two," he says. "The third one isn't here."

He introduces them in turn, a Touched grenadier and an Aqueian alchemist, and I can assume they're real people after a couple of minutes of talk. He's already given them the in-game privileges he can, so I take care of the rest of ops as we chat, the maps and raid schedules and the directory. It's Regnava's turn after that, and she only has one, a Touched aquamancer, also a real human being (and, it turns out, Vietnamese and preferring French to English, so we end up chatting about that for a while).

I haven't kept Krozin waiting that long: fifteen minutes at most. But while I'm introducing the new player to the other non-native English speakers in the fief, a text chat window pops up.

SACHEM*C: *I've been watching the audio on the remaning knights*

SACHEM*C: **Remaining*

FATIGUEE*D: *And?*

SACHEM*C: *They're antsy.*

FATIGUEE*D: *But they're real people?*

SACHEM*C: *All but three of the feeds have activity.*

"Krozin," I say into the microphone, "present your knights."

"Knights," Krozin says, "present your arms."

It's not the first time someone's tried to kill me. It's the first time thirty people have tried to kill me simultaneously. The monitor floods with menus and health bars as we're plunged into combat, and Fatiguee's bar is dropped to half in the first ten seconds. Two spells and four gunshots plus one smoke grenade, and the dais is a gray and gold smear of graphic design and violence.

I won't have time to get a spell off if another one of these barrages hits. I don't even know who's on my side, so I can't shout orders onto an open feed.

I am *fucked*.

Sachem blasts through Krozin's line, his war fan slicing through the smoke. No joke, Orin shouts, "My Lady!" into the mic. "I'll hold them! Do what you need to do!"

He means cast, so I click in the commands for a Rule of Might spell. All the hostiles are close enough to freeze, if Sachem and his knights hold the line.

I cast, and the timer starts running. Twenty seconds. Regnava takes a lightning bolt that was clearly meant for me. Someone starts throwing group heals around, but I don't know *whose group*. Orin drops two of Krozin's knights off the field with his war fan, but they blink right back in. Resurrection relics? Where the hell did Krozin get those? Fuck, probably from the raid they were just on.

It goes without saying that they planned this. I'd really appreciate knowing *why*.

Regnava drops. So does the new Vietnamese player. Sachem gets smacked with Tarnish, then Poison and Blind. Five more seconds. Hold that line for five more seconds, Orin, please—

Krozin shoves him aside, raises his gun, and sighs, clear through my headset, "I hoped you'd put up more of a fight."

In the *Annals of Altestis*, it will be written that he popped a cap in Fatiguee's face, except in appropriately Elizabethan language.

The *eternal* part of *Eternal Reign* is, yes, a misnomer, but if death were permanent in a universe this competitive, no one would play. In the earliest days of the game, respawn points were simply semiregulated neutral zones, usually in urban centers run directly by the Council of Gerents. If a character was killed without a resurrection relic on hand, she reverted to her most recent backup and lost anywhere from five to a hundred minutes of game time while her soul was reconnected. In that lapse of time, who or whatever killed her would run rampant over her holdings and take anything that wasn't nailed down, but all would otherwise be well.

Of course, the system was too simple to last and too fun to break. Players began to lurk outside the respawn points waiting to enact vendettas and visit aggro on recently reborn players trying to get back to their demesnes. Half hour lapses became day-long losses became complete losses as the resurrected characters became effectively trapped. The Council of Gerents was, if not deaf to their pleas, not precisely timely in its restitution.

So the players responded by counter-gaming the system. Somewhat literal protection rackets formed: characters could pay caravans and bodyguards to escort them home from the respawn points. It wasn't free—and the better the protection, the more you could expect to pay—but for a time, it wasn't prohibitively expensive and was reasonably trustworthy.

Then the counter-counter-gaming started. Players with vendettas would form sleeper cells in common rackets. Scammers would transfer soul contracts or respawning rights, or worse, auction them off. An underground soul trade played right into the hands of some of the particularly devious pirates, and characters could strand recently resurrected players so far from home that they'd have to start over from scratch—or worse, characters could coordinate coups like the one I just fucking experienced to maximize the amount of time pillaging the victim's holdings.

The Council of Gerents finally came through about six months into this fiasco. Two important, world-warping changes were made to the general gameplay to offset the drama. First, the head of the most powerful and consistent of the protection guilds, Doctor Conesto, was elevated to vicegerent, giving her full mod privileges and rendering her immortal. Conesto's racket thus became a generally perfect trust, and any player contract with them would be honored. Contracts would be priced based on distance from respawn to fief, or from respawn to neutral if you couldn't afford the entire journey. And if you fucked with Conesto, she'd fuck with you right back. It worked appreciably well for most players and, perhaps paramount to the Council of Gerents, prevented people from leaving the game en masse.

But for some characters, it wasn't enough. Some, like my Fatiguee, were too far out from any respawn points for Conesto to make much of a difference. Others, like raiders and pirates, weren't comfortable turning up in the urban centers with wanted posters and dukesguards ready and waiting. Others still wanted a means of controlling where their souls would rise so as to avoid the rackets altogether. And for them, the council provided reliquaries.

For ten thousand dubloons, you could buy a portable and exclusive respawn point, a literal soul jar. A reliquary you could save a backup to at any time (again, for a fee) and place anywhere you deemed safe. Or in the hands of any *person* you deemed safe. The council will not be held liable for any accidents or poor decisions you make in transferring your reliquary, but the option now exists, and that's important.

Count Sachem and Duchess Fatiguee exchanged reliquaries immediately after purchase. Fatiguee placed Sachem's in her port city Delitien; Sachem held Fatiguee's in his home keep, Lowslip. We're a little farther from each other than I'd prefer, but at least I have a castle, and Orin's not the one they want dead again when I respawn in fifteen minutes.

Fatiguee's most recent backup was made right after I won the contest, so that's no problem for me. I've only lost Altestis itself.

CHAPTER THREE

I adore Orin, but:

PLAYER HARASSMENT: FAIR OR UNFAIR?

Hey guys, Orin from Aqueabilitas here. Unfortunately, I won't be bringing you our scheduled Q&A session today, because I have a much more serious issue to address. Bear with me. Or better yet, don't, and be just as pissed off at the unfairness as I am.

As most of you know, I'm an *Eternal Reign* player and I've stood behind the gameplay freedoms of this saltwater sandbox since the game's creation. I believed that by providing an avenue for gamers to engage in a fully player-created and -understood environment, ER could become a fruitful platform for examination of the gaming community. The mods have extremely limited influence on ER, basically enough to keep subscriptions from plummeting, and while there are always people who will take advantage of that for personal gain (c.f. the Respawn drama several months ago and Eightgate last year), to my knowledge it's been confined to the game itself until now.

Note the use of the past tense.

A little over a week ago, the ER design team announced a contest winner. The terms of the contest were basic bluebooking and record-keeping of the player-driven storyline, and Duchess Fatiguee of Altestis was determined the winner. Immediately afterwards, Duchess Fatiguee received what I can only describe as an onslaught of verbal and textual harassment. The constant messaging drove her off the server for a time and prevented her from fulfilling her demesne responsibilities (in ER if you hold enough ships or castles to be a count or a duke, you need to work to keep them). And her own knights and counts took this opportunity to mount a coup against her as soon as she reappeared, and *booted her out of her own fief.*

Now, some of you will say this is par for the course in ER, and that it's a classic high-risk/high-reward situation. If this had been something entirely motivated in-game, I'd agree with you. It wasn't. This was a carefully calculated succession of opportunities to undermine a player, not a character, *based on out-of-game events.*

That is despicable. It's hitting below the belt. It's *I Have Your Wife.* It's Tonya Harding levels of bullshit. Someone—a *cadre* of someones, conspired to oust a player from a game. Because what? Because she won a contest and they *didn't? How childish can we be?*

What happens in Vegas stays in Vegas, and what happens in a game should stay in the game. But that usually includes some form of protection against people taking advantage of out-of-game factors to progress in-game. In professional sports, when there's an injury on the field, play stops. In competitive gaming, everything from heckling to epileptic fits stops the action. In multiplayer games, everyone has the right to pause, and it's considered good form to honor that pause. Hell, *in the cesspool that is video poker* there are rules of engagement.

Not so in ER. Any rules at all would be considered infringing *on the rights of the players.*

I believe it is possible to have a game in which the players follow rules even if the characters don't. The ER design team does as well—enough to answer the petitions of the players when their characters keep dying. There *is* separation and it *should* be enforced. Because on any other platform, when people pursue real-world vendettas in a game, it's unsportsmanlike conduct and punishable by removal.

I'm arguing that this is another such oversight and the design team of *Eternal Reign* and future games like it should take responsibility: since certainly we must enforce a standard of *player behavior* as distinct from *character behavior*, how are we to enforce it if some people just can't be decent human beings?

ETA 17:43 EST: Speaking of people who can't be decent human beings, the mods have now turned IP logging on for this post and instituted captcha.

Comments (1252)

Sigmund Frood
Easy. Leave the game.

Orin
I do believe you missed the point of my article.

> **Sigmund Frood**
> I do believe you missed the point of ER.
>
> It's a player-created system, not a character-created system. Characters can't create anything. They wouldn't exist without us. Therefore the rules are about player conduct, and the point, which you missed, is that ER has no rules. If you can't take the heat, stay out of the kitchen.
>
> > **Orin**
> > If the kitchen's on fire, get a friend with a hose.
> >
> > There are already rules in place for players of ER. There's a terms of service agreement, which is effectively a contract between the players and SummerStorm. There are gameplay mechanics, which obey conventions of their own. And on four separate occasions since ER came out, the creative team has updated the environment to contribute to the welfare of the players, and as reparation for their unforeseen oversights. I'm arguing that this is another such oversight and the design team should take responsibility. If they won't take responsibility, then the players should, but I have a feeling that's too much to ask.
> >
> > > **hOlywEll**
> > > no shit sherlock
> > >
> > > **Raeg Quitt**
> > > Use another finger, Watson!

Sigmund Frood

It's not a game for people who want to play nice. It's a game for people who want to play by their own rules. The players aren't accountable for their actions, period. If they become accountable, the game loses its appeal.

Nyan Dere

why not think of it like larping or improv? anything illegal you do to a player should be punishable, but anything illegal you do to a character is fine.

Sigmund Frood

It's a slippery slope. Once you decide that things you do to the player are punishable, every pussy out there will start screaming about how unsafe they feel and slapping trigger warnings on everything. There is no point in a player-driven game if the PC police are running it.

(Show 14 more comments)

Hiafartha

Fag spotted!

Orin

Troll spotted!
Troll *banned*!

Code Red Breakah

In theory I agree, but haters gon hate and killas gon kill. The dudes at SummerStorm knew what they were doing when they made a sandbox and opened it to the public.

Orin

If they knew entirely what they were doing, they'd have created a perfect system. The system isn't perfect, ergo, no, they didn't know what they were doing. The system is evolving based on player contribution.

Code Red Breakah

Killas are players too. They're just making the game they want to play.

Orin

If the game they want to play involves hurting actual human beings, they should go hang out by the punch bowl with Jigsaw. In jail.

abednego

if fatiguee is gonna fold over something as trivial as a coup she shouldn't be playing ER

like

she should go write her fifty shades of grey bullshit elsewhere

win/win

Orin

First of all, and most importantly, she did not leave because of the coup. She took a break because of the harassment, which affects the player, not the character. Fatiguee's player has been involved in ER since it came out, and other MMOs and MUDs long before that. She can and has taken in-game actions in stride. Again, she has retreated not because she can't take the game, but because people are coming after *her*. There is a difference.

Second, it's not *Fifty Shades of Grey*. It is event bluebooking, and Altestis has been home to the most elaborate courtiering game I have ever seen in my fifteen years of online gaming. She was awarded for writing down events that transpired in her domain in a fashion that the dev team found entertaining. More importantly, it was a contest, and they asked *everyone who submitted* to novelize their experiences. It was a novelization contest! A courtiering game is extremely complex and just as valid to novelize as a financial game, raiding, trading, escorting, alchemitizing, piracy, or any of the other things you can do in ER. If you condemn her for taking advantage of the same freedoms that you insist must persist, you're hypocritical in the extreme.

abednego
oh now i get it

you're her fucktoy in the annals
she gonna split the prize with you after she rides your dick?

shadrach
Dude this white knight ain't got a dick. She fucks him in the ass with hers.

Orin
Congratulations, you're both banned.

So is Meshach if he shows up.

Miserable Pile
HOLY SHIT THAT IS NERDY AS FUCK

Plasma Snake
Dude, seriously? Three people banned already over some girl who ragequit because she can't handle smacktalk?

Orin

No, three people banned already for using defamatory language pertaining to my sexuality, insinuating that Fatiguee's player is trading sex for support, and speculating on specific sex acts that are none of their business.

21guns

dude

chill

O Laura O

You're right, the situation is despicable, and I hope Fatiguee's player is taking care of herself right now. She's lucky to have a friend like you who's trying to understand what's going on for her, and you raise a lot of good points, but I think you're missing part of the picture.

Fatiguee's player is female. That's all the excuse some of these ass clowns need. This harassment isn't occurring in a vacuum, and the sheer amount of vitriol that certain dude-bros have for gamers who don't look like them is, frankly, terrifying. It's driven me off servers in the past, and cut off avenues for my friends in every corner of the gaming world. And unfortunately, while *Eternal Reign* is a great platform to test new forms of social interaction, it's also an incubator for the same old bullshit.

I've got a couple of articles on the previous instances of OOC harrassment on my blog, and a few by my friend Jahata on Afrofuturist Micronation. She's playing ZxA instead now, but I'm testing some community-control measures on my *Eternal Reign* server if you're interested in stats and anecdata.

strawhatcrew

The afrofascists have arrived!

mxxstep
and with them godwin

red the blood
if you really liked this guy you wouldnt comment on his posts now we've got him too you fat black whore

go back to afrofascist micropenis

> **Orin**
> Banned.

Orin
Thanks for your support. I've read a couple of your friend's articles before, and yours look interesting as well. I didn't think it was my place to comment before (I try very hard not to be that kind of Nice Guy), and I'll admit that the magnitude of harassment you and your friend have described didn't seem real until it happened to someone close to me. I also know that I'm coming from a different position and have a different audience, even if the trolls spawned under the same bridge. Chivalry means using your privilege for good, after all. If there's anything I can promote to help you, I'd be happy to.

By all means, email me with the server info and your community stats. I think my lady would love to know there's someone else out there pushing the bounds of ER's capability.

> **21guns**
> gonna be sick

O Laura O
On the record, and in the interest of public discussion, I don't think our audiences are so different. We're trying to change the same world, after all!

I appreciate you putting thought into when your input is needed though, and it probably wasn't on any of Jahata's posts back then, so thank you. But in this situation, and in this forum, I definitely appreciate your ideas. It's your house. I just dropped a pamphlet at your door.

We can take this to email.

HIGHLIGHTS
AND THE BEDROOM

> **Orin**
> Banned.

166rhys
afrofascist feminazi seduces beta kyke fuckboy

film at eleven

> **Orin**
> Banned.

whenimgon
lay off the ban-hammer thor

you jerk it too much it'll never grow back

> **Orin**
> Banned.

nonny noh
we can do this all day you fat turd

(Show 68 more comments)

(View 293 more threads)

So. That happened.
I adore Orin. But.

CHAPTER FOUR

There are a million other things I could be doing. There are a dozen other things I *should* be doing. There's a whole world outside this apartment that I'm supposed to take by storm; talents I've honed for years across two continents lying in wait to be shared; contacts to forge and shows to see and ticket lines to stand in so I can make the most of living my twenties in this beautiful, bustling city full of ambition and nerve.

Instead, I am hunting purple kelp.

Said kelp can only be gathered two ways, and one involves deep-sea mining equipment that Bannedict can't afford yet (and frankly if he could afford it, I wouldn't need the mutant alginate in the first place). Therefore I have spent the better part of three hours tracking the migration of pepinsharks through kelp-infested waters, trapping said sharks, removing the kelp from their dorsal fins, and releasing the sharks back into the wild to preserve the delicate ecosystem.

I wonder if any of these skills are more marketable than acting? Probably. There are pirates in Somalia. Maybe they need a French interpreter. Or a piratical maid-of-all-work. I could do that. Or I could forage reams of virtual kelp.

The choice is easy.

It's four in the morning. Alain should be coming back from the bars soon, and Jackie's light stopped creeping under the door an hour ago. When I checked at midnight, Orin was still feeding the trolls. There aren't quite two thousand comments yet, but close. Aqueabilitas articles usually get ten, twenty max. I try not to read them.

Well, as Yoda says, "*Faire, ou pas. 'Essayez' ne pas exister.*" It's much punchier in English. It's also much better advice in English, because clearly I didn't take it in French. The comments suck me in like a lubricated wormhole and, since Orin's busy dealing with them, there's no point in prying him away to strategize about what the hell we're doing about Altestis. He can blow off some steam and fight his righteous fight. I can hunt purple kelp.

Well, now the trolls have their confirmation that Fatiguee's player is female. Whether that's true or not.

As if nuance matters at all on the internet.

My world shrunk to this room hours ago, and it's down to the size of the screen. For all that *Eternal Reign* purports to be an age of expansion and a boundless ocean, at this moment I could plausibly put it in my pocket.

A text hail pops up like laundry change.

UHRUU*D*: *East coast midnight oil?*

I wish I'd been this conscientious with my players in Altestis. If they'd have all felt as warm and consoled as I do right now, I mean. It probably wouldn't work in a courtiering game where everyone is currying favor with one hotkey and stabbing me in the back with the other. But a hail from Duchess Uhruu in her kelp-starved convoy is music to my headset.

BANNEDICT: *kelp farming and insomnia*

BANNEDICT: *not the ideal combination*

UHRUU*D*: *I completely understand. I'm in it for the long haul tonight myself.*

BANNEDICT: *if i may?*

UHRUU*D*: *May what, ask why?*

BANNEDICT: *yes*

BANNEDICT: *sorry*

UHRUU*D*: *Asking is always fine. And the answer, this time, is a combination of caffeine and internet drama.*

BANNEDICT: *say it isn;t so*

UHRUU*D*: *Not my drama, fortunately. Did you hear about the novelization contest?*

Oh *fuck me with a hamster and an elderberry branch.* Laura. O Laura O. The class act who responded courteously to Orin's article and is writing posts about her own experiences with harassment. Wait, maybe not. It could be someone else. It's a common name and there are a hundred thousand people playing this game, and fuck, this virtual shark has no kelp on it.

Well, I could tell the truth right here and confess that I'm not a guy, which would make her drama seem all about me and completely override her feelings *and* make Orin look like an asshole. Or I could keep my trap shut.

Once again, the choice is easy. All these either/or, yes/no, black/white choices are so fucking easy.

BANNEDICT: *yeah kind of*

BANNEDICT: *that court game won?*

I am scum. I am the mop bucket at the escargot farm. But it's the correct thing to do. She wants everyone on the new server to feel safe, and Fatiguee is not safe. I am not safe.

UHRUU*D*: *Yeah. Then her counts turned against her and spammed her off the server. According to one of her allies it's a full mutiny and they took her home keep.*

BANNEDICT: *that's gross*

Say I, in the ironic understatement of the century.

UHRUU*D*: *The ally count posted a PSA about it on Aqueabilitas if you want the link.*

BANNEDICT: *sure*

UHRUU*D*: *http://bit.ly/sdhk22i3n Usual warning about not reading the comments. There's some amazingly racist and homophobic bullshit in there.*

If only she knew. Well, she does know. She all but admitted that she's the Laura from the comments section.

UHRUU*D*: *I've been in emails with the count, he's got a few good ideas. He said he's going to hold the fort until the gerents do something about the trolls.*

BANNEDICT: *gotta admire that*

Not that he told me. And it's my fief. But clearly it's more important to Orin to hold the line and make his point, and I can support that. It's not like I'm logging on to Fatiguee again any time soon.

UHRUU*D*: *To a point. Cis straight dude, so the trolls aren't going to be as nasty as they were to me or his duchess. But at least he knows it, and he's planning on using it to his advantage. In my experience people like him have a better success rate at translating our grievances into a* *form these troglodytes can understand. I'm not sure how I feel about that, but as long as he owns up to it I think he can avoid mansplaining.*

BANNEDICT: *you've dealt with this a lot?*

UHRUU*D*: *On every game I've ever played.*

BANNEDICT: *you're really tough*

UHRUU*D*: *Stubborn, I think.*

BANNEDICT: *maybe*

BANNEDICT: *i'd call it toughness*

BANNEDICT: *my roommates dealt with the same thing when we were kids*

BANNEDICT: *got out as soon as they could*

BANNEDICT: *one's an algerian drag queen*

BANNEDICT: *he sticks to jrpgs now, ultimate odyssey, you know the drill*

UHRUU*D*: *Yeah, I can definitely see why he'd swear off MMOs in this climate.*

BANNEDICT: *the other's a butch boi*

BANNEDICT: *i don't think she got harassed, exactly*

BANNEDICT: *more like she dipped a toe in and discovered a saltwater allergy*

UHRUU*D*: *So it's neither her beautiful house nor her beautiful wife.*

BANNEDICT: *haha apter than you know*

BANNEDICT: *shes always felt better in weaboo country*

BANNEDICT: *especially with fanfic and all that's a matriarchal society*

BANNEDICT: *sororial maybe*

UHRUU*D*: *Yeah, because when men write fanfic it gets multi-million dollar production deals and they call it Wicked.*

Dare I hope? Dare I dream? I type before I can stop my fingers.

BANNEDICT: *dare i hope you're a theatre nerd?*

UHRUU*D*: *If you get invited to my gramma's place you can clock my family's cast album collection. On vinyl.*

Oh my god. *I have been changed for good.* This is some Stanislavsky method fodder right here, because my heart just rose up into my throat and started beating the walls like the Blue Man Group. All of the Broadway ballads I ever learned are competing for space in my head in two different languages and far too many keys. Tony pines for Maria, Marius and Cosette chirp sweet nothings from opposite sides of the garden fence, Tuptim and Lun Tha kiss in a shadow—

UHRUU*D*: *You there, Daphnis?*

—and I am a lying piece of shit.

BANNEDICT: *sorry*

BANNEDICT: *kelp quest*

BANNEDICT: *that's awesome though*

BANNEDICT: *are you an actress?*

UHRUU*D*: *I tried in LA for a while after college but got sick of getting cast as whores and housekeeping. I do a little community theater now but I don't have the bug, you know?*

BANNEDICT: *yeah*

UHRUU*D*: *What about you? Backstage or on it?*

BANNEDICT: *neither, these days*

BANNEDICT: *but i'm an actor in nyc*

BANNEDICT: *corps mostly, some film and tv work*

BANNEDICT: *but if i had a regular paying job i wouldn't be playing mmos at 4 am*

BANNEDICT: *not that i'm accusing you of not having a job*

BANNEDICT: *sorry*

UHRUU*D*: *It's fine, I didn't think you were.*

BANNEDICT: *may i ask what your day job is?*

UHRUU*D*: *You can always ask. And I'm in my second year of law school.*

BANNEDICT: *no shit*

BANNEDICT: *that's awesome*

UHRUU*D*: *Yeah, I'm gonna give them the old Razzle Dazzle.*

BANNEDICT: *oh god i have chicago lyrics for my agent's ringtone*

UHRUU*D*: *Sweet!*

BANNEDICT: *so will it be criminal law or are you still in the eclectic stage*

UHRUU*D*: *Not sure, but given what I've been through I think it's a good time to get into IP law. It intersects with civil rights law in a lot of interesting places and, well, I want to be in the room where it happens.*

BANNEDICT: *oh my god, not you too*

UHRUU*D*: *Guilty as charged! Did you get to see Hamilton live?*

BANNEDICT: *nope, can't afford tickets*

BANNEDICT: *debating whether to sell one or both kidneys*

BANNEDICT: *one of my roommates saw it off-broadway but I was out of town*

BANNEDICT: *so i'm in the same boat as you*

UHRUU*D*: *It'll come out here eventually. I'll just make do with the mixtape until then.*

BANNEDICT: *out here being?*

UHRUU*D*: *Seattle. Actually, I'm holding a panel at GeeKon in a couple months on marginalized people in the gaming community. If you know anyone local, they should come!*

BANNEDICT: *oh right*

She's a superlative human being. She's a gamer and a theater nerd. She quotes *Hamilton*. And she's going to be at GeeKon when I ostensibly accept my prize for winning the novelization contest, which she doesn't know I won, because she thinks I'm a man.

BANNEDICT: *i may be going*

I am a superlative idiot.

BANNEDICT: *i'll keep you posted*

UHRUU*D*: *Great! Please do.*

Maybe it won't be so difficult after all. I can drop the *Actually, I am Fatiguee!* bomb a few weeks into this and just say I didn't feel ready. Or I can admit to it at the con when we're a little closer. All those romantic misunderstandings, you know. Act one peril. As long as I take care of it before someone notices the gun on the mantelpiece, we should make it out of *The Seagull* intact.

UHRUU*D*: *And I'm thinking of inviting that count I told you about.*

I need to work on my timing.

BANNEDICT: *what*

BANNEDICT: *orin?*

UHRUU*D*: *You know him?*

BANNEDICT: *yeah*

BANNEDICT: *i recognized him when you linked the article*

BANNEDICT: *we were in the same guild a few games back*

That is a complete technical truth. No polygraph would pick it up. We *were* in the same guild a few games back. We're just *still* in the same guild. And if I dig myself any deeper I'll hit groundwater.

UHRUU*D*: *Excellent. I'm glad you can vet him! He's a class act.*

Is this how Nice Guys feel? Because I hope this is how Nice Guys feel. Because it feels like *crap*.

CHAPTER FIVE

Hair day is a production around here. All three musketqueers get involved, because if we didn't, I'd be a brunette, Alain's weaves would wind up in the dishwasher, and Jackie would lose the security deposit.

So we have converted the apartment into a cheap knockoff harem, except instead of lounging cushions we have scrap towels covering every remotely valuable surface. Everyone is bare to the waist or more—Jackie's Jackie—with Saran Wrap turbans to hold the dye in. The kitchen is peppered with vile concoctions that the world considers aphrodisiacs. Jackie's steaming bowl of henna mixed with coconut oil and, I shit you not, eighty dollar Turkish honey, sits on a double-boiler on the front burner. My toner and bleach and cheap conditioner have taken over the kitchen table and three tupperware tubs. In addition to twenty feet of ombre extensions drip-dying on the fire escape, Alain is working on four wigs on four Styrofoam heads clamped to the coffee table, and is adding a few new streaks to his actual hair. He's currently in possession of a paint palette, eight different candy-colored bottles of dye, salt, ethanol, a cauldron of boiling water, newspaper, a hairdryer, two iPads with reference images, and ancient rubber gloves that look like a serial killer just brutalized the entire cast of *My Little Pony*.

Since Jackie's the quickest and has the least to do, she gets to choose the entertainment. While Alain gets his Mother Gothel on, she and I are sprawled (carefully) on the couch. I didn't catch the title of this particular anime; it involves Catholic schoolgirls and roses and lesbian drama, so that's a point in its favor. But if I don't pay attention,

I can't follow along: this edition has English subtitles, but no French dub, and my Japanese is virtually nonexistent. Which leaves me lost every time I check my phone.

Spam. Spam. Newsletter from my casting agency about a workshop like all other workshops. Notification of royalty payments from that one film that did well at Cannes, not that my Featured Extra role contributed to reviews. Stage combat class schedule. Spam. Facebook update for a thread I'm not participating in. Spam. Backstage.com native advertisement.

Alain shouts at one of the wigs for not holding a part. Jackie turns up the volume. Japanese Catholic schoolgirls have drama. I switch accounts.

Fatiguee's email isn't much more interesting than mine. Spam. Spam. *Eternal Reign* subscription automatic payment stub. Announcement of scheduled server downtime this weekend, two hours. Spam. Something labeled *Controversy*.

Who the hell uses *Controversy* as a subject line?

FROM: Publicity (publicity@summerstorm.net)
TO: Fatiguee Altestis (je.suis.fatiguee@qmail.com)

SUBJECT: Controversy

> *Fatiguee,*
> *It has come to SummerStorm's attention that despite your victory in the novelization contest, you haven't had much player activity. The gerents on your server have recorded only one hour of logged-in play under your account over the past week, and only three hours the week before. While we know that real-world engagements come up and take precedence over game commitments, we cannot help but be concerned that it sends the wrong message to the hundreds of others who participated in the contest, when the winner is no longer a participant. We would appreciate if you allayed these concerns.*
>
> *In addition, we have been made aware that a man claiming to be one of your counts has begun a crusade in your honor and is implicating the design staff of Eternal Reign for alleged harassment. This is poor form for a contest winner who intends to meet with the design team.*

Of course if your absence can be explained by extenuating circumstances we will not hold it against you. If not, please resume play, or relinquish your title in favor of the runner-up.

Thank you,
Malcolm Harding
Publicity, SummerStorm Entertainment Inc.
FRATRES AD SCORTA

They have got to be kidding me. The world has got to be kidding me.

As far as I know, I have an entirely legitimate excuse for not logging on, and the documentation to prove it. Screencaps and all. And he can't really fault me for taking time off in the hopes that this bullshit blows over, after my own court game blew up in my face.

One of Alain's dye bottles chooses that moment to explode. Fuck, speaking of blowing up in my face. Looks like a job for a French maid!

I clean while Alain salvages the wigs and Jackie shuffles the towels and newspapers around. Once that's done, it's about time for me to rinse out my bleach mix. My feats of self-delusion persist through a quick but thorough shower, after which I *must* consider how to respond to such a ridiculous email.

On the one hand, this publicity guy is only partly aware of the situation. Alleged harassment. To him, it *is* alleged because I have the screencaps and he doesn't. The file is enormous, but I could send him a sampler platter. And explain that it's not ER's fault, it's the players being a collective bag of dicks. Politely, though. And I'll give him the other hand, since he's probably just covering his ass. Liability. A poorly worded check-in.

I can reply to him while I let my hair sit before the toner. Jackie scoots over to let me back on the couch, the Japanese Catholic schoolgirl lesbians have their reams of drama, and I deal with mine.

DE: Fatiguee Altestis (je.suis.fatiguee@qmail.com)
POUR: Publicity (publicity@summerstorm.net)

SUJET: RE: Controversy

> *Thank you for your concern. There is no need to take away my victory.*
>   *It has been difficult to play ER because of the volume of harassment I continue to receive, but I will make an effort to log more hours. I have assembled a file of screencaps indicating that the harassment is not alleged and will send them to you if you require proof. As a duchess I am unable to turn off messaging entirely because I must be available to my players. The trolls take advantage of this and have flooded my inbox with several hundred messages per day, utilizing over a thousand different user accounts. Sifting through these messages for the concerns of my knights and counts is exhausting and does not afford me time to pursue character quests. Furthermore, as the recent coup attests, it renders me vulnerable because I cannot assess my own supposed allies. If ER staff would institute a Report Abuse function and address this issue I would have an easier time resuming play.*
>   *The post made by Orin at Aqueabilitas does not accuse ER staff of committing the harassment. I think his concern is the behavior of the players, which ER permits or encourages. This is not the same thing. I do not think it is poor form to raise concerns in a public forum, and while he uses my experience as an example, it is his post, not mine.*
>   *As the annals attest, I enjoy ER greatly and have spent two years as part of its growing community of players. Please address this issue so I may continue to enjoy it.*
>   *Her Grace the Duchess Fatiguee*

There, that seems sensible enough. I can and do set my phone down and get back to work on my hair. I should probably cut it soon. Or ask Alain to do it. When he isn't busy with the Technicolor topiaries.

Once I've mixed the toner, I carry it, gloves, and a spackler out to Jackie and tap her on the shoulder. "Roots?"

"Sure." She smiles and slides a little forward on the couch so I can sit down on the floor in front of her leg, and gives my scalp a quick scratch, then pulls on the gloves and gets started.

"How's your arm?"

She tugs on my hair with her left hand by way of an answer. It's been about a week since her last tattoo session, and the bandages are off—otherwise it couldn't be hair day—so the outlines of hundreds of art-nouveau roses stand out clear and proud. "Coloring starts when we get back from Seattle," she says.

Wait. "'We'?"

"They approved my panels this morning." She massages toner into my roots. "And I got us a room at the con hotel."

"I thought they were all sold out." When I booked mine two weeks ago, I had to go to one of the adjacent hotels. It's within walking distance, and inexpensive in comparison, but still not at the center of GeeKon activity.

"Only the con-rate ones. I paid standard."

Jackie can afford that. I guess if we're splitting it, I can contribute. "How much do I—"

"Let her," Alain sings from the kitchen. "Also I need to know what flight you're on."

"You too?"

"Turns out they have a cosplay drag show and there's room for Ivy to make her plane ticket back." He holds up one of the wigs, a lime-green confection that looks right out of *Jem and the Holograms*, and gives the ends a flick. "Summoner Lydia's all grown up, and there's a Mist Dragon in her pants."

"Or she's just happy to see you," Jackie adds.

"Oh my god." I try not to laugh too much because then I'll get toner all over my face, and lean against Jackie's knees to compensate. "I mean it though, Jackie, you shouldn't pay for me."

"It's a gift," she says firmly. "You won a contest. They should have given you more than a badge."

They have. They've given me a superlative headache and about fourteen sleepless nights. "Still—"

She twists my hair and tucks it into a plastic bag so the dye will set. "Go cancel yours."

"And get the flight info," Alain adds.

Well, that's a clear order. I grab my phone and thumb into email. Never mind that I was seriously considering *not* going, and never mind that the SummerStorm staff is apparently reconsidering my victory. I can't prevent Jackie and Alain from enjoying GeeKon.

And, as I have spoken of the devil, he has appeared in my inbox.

FROM: Publicity (publicity@summerstorm.net)
TO: Fatiguee Altestis (je.suis.fatiguee@qmail.com)

SUBJECT: RE: Controversy

There is no need to send screencaps. As a Report Abuse function would likely be misused, we have no intention of instituting one. We advise you to block messages from any account you wish. Eternal Reign is not liable for player behavior. Gamers will be gamers and competition is a fact of life. Perhaps the instigators of the coup believe that a negligent and cowardly player should not have the responsibilities of a duchess.

Essentially, if you want to defend your realm, defend it. If you can't, you can't. That's the way of the game.

Malcolm Harding
Publicity, SummerStorm Entertainment Inc.
FRATRES AD SCORTA

. . . That fucking *assclown.*

Well, I got Alain and Jackie the flight info. By some miracle, there was room on mine for one of them, even though we won't be sitting together. Alain took the seat, probably so I can help him lug around his suitcases and wig boxes, and Jackie snagged herself a slightly later flight with no layover that gets in around the same time.

I am locked in. I am going to GeeKon, whether SummerStorm will see me or not.

If I'm going out to Seattle, I might as well try to do what SummerStorm says. Be less cowardly. Block what I need to block. Keep building a file of bullshit so radioactive the aliens who colonize Earth in the future will be able to accurately date its fossilized remains. If *Monsieur Publicité* won't look, maybe whoever meets me at GeeKon will.

So I log on. I'll hop over to Bannedict later. I can commit to screencapping and blocking one hundred assholes. *Take the heat. Defend the realm. Don't be a coward.*

Five thousand seven hundred ninety-two messages since the coup. If I said that aloud in French it would take two breaths.

I can do this. I have to do this.

The first fifteen are a litany of sex crimes to pursue upon my alternately living and dead body. The sixteenth is a notification of a new knight, but Krozin has already approved it. The next ten mostly pertain to various orifices and things I can shove down them, or up them, and the subsequent two merely insist that I commit suicide. Someone has also taken care to send me *Annals* fanart, though it's somewhat crudely drawn and involves a great deal more blunt force trauma than I'd prefer. Then two new knight requests, which Krozin has also taken care of approving.

A lot of these are invites, actually. And Krozin's approved them all. He's letting the trolls in. He's making them his knights. He's reinforcing Altestis with dozens—maybe hundreds—of players determined to keep me out.

I can't stop him. He controls the server. All I can do is fight back.

Screencap, save, block. Screencap, save, block. Lather. Rinse. Repeat.

Something smells like burning.

I'm still wearing a plastic bag on my head.

Oh *fuck*. My hair.

CHAPTER SIX

"Hey," Orin says.

"Hey yourself." I try to hold the phone on my left ear. The skin burns are more on the right side, and it serves me right. I didn't lose much. I can part the hair to hide the bald spot and the rest is a few shades lighter than I'd prefer, but hey, silver hair is in now. I don't know how I'm going to explain it to my agent. I may not explain it at all and just wait for things to grow out.

Alain said I look like a JRPG villain. I'm inclined to agree. Meanwhile I'm lying on my bed with an abused scalp and a headache for the ages.

Orin coughs into the speaker. "Everything okay? Sorry," he corrects, "stupid question."

"No, it's a good question. Maybe phrasing it as 'Is everything more not-okay or less not-okay than it was?' makes more sense. I don't know."

He laughs, humorless but sweet. "*More not-okay* sounds misleadingly cheerful. But that's what it is, isn't it?"

"Yeah. SummerStorm emailed me. They're thinking of revoking the victory."

"They can't do that!"

"It's their game. They can do whatever they want." And honestly, I should have seen this coming. All success is fleeting. All casting is at the discretion of the director. There is always someone else they wanted waiting to step in when you fail to live up to their expectations. "And it gets worse."

"Worse how?"

"Krozin has ops. I signed on to try to block the trolls and it turns out he's inviting them. Or at least taking them in once they sign up."

"This is *unconscionable*." Orin sounds more righteously indignant than I feel, which is par for the course but still kind of hurtful. I called him to strategize, not complain. "There's got to be something staff will do about this."

"If there is, I haven't thought of it. And *Monsieur Publicité* is a real cavalier," I add. Sarcasm is easier in English.

"What did he say?"

"Here, give me a second." I put him on speaker, then forward him the email. "There." I flop back on the pillow, which pulls my chemical-burned scalp tight. "*Merde.*"

"Daphne?"

"It's fine, just hit my head." He doesn't have to know about me fucking up my hair because of this ridiculousness. "More not-okay."

"I wish I could hold you right now," he says. "No one should have to go through this, least of all you."

Thank god he went on so I can ignore the first part. "I'm sure other people have it worse." Like Laura.

"It's not a matter of worse or better. No one should have to lose something they love because of judgmental idiots. Wait, the email just arrived."

While he reads it, I just listen to him breathe. Maybe I can't ignore the first part of what he said entirely. I'd love to curl up with someone, someone real and warm and strong. Maybe not Orin—not now, at any rate—but someone who'd line up with me and just *be*, someone to take up my space and I'll take up theirs and we could both be real, together. Real because of each other.

"How dare he," Orin says, and that snaps me clean out of my reverie. "If I sent an email like that to a student I'd be fired on the spot."

"It's not school," I remind him. "It's a game with no rules."

"Well, maybe it shouldn't be."

"Orin—"

"I won't write to him. But I will write to someone else on the site and ask if we can get moved to another server or whatever. Or if there's a way to censure Krozin."

"We?"

"Where my lady goes, I go," he says, in complete seriousness. As far as I can tell, at any rate.

Why is the divide so blurry? Why is this game taking over my real world?

Oh, right. Because I let it.

I don't mind Orin's sentiment. Not exactly. But, "Can we talk about something else?"

"Sure. It'll take me some time to find the right person to send the request to."

"How's the dissertation?"

"Anything but that, ha." There, that's better: he's on the spot instead of me. "If I don't finish another chapter before the holidays, I won't have time after them."

"How many is this?"

"It's like writing a book. This is four. Chapter four. But four chapters in means something different depending on if you're Plato or Hegel."

"And which are you?"

"The outline says eight, so somewhere in between."

I'll have to look up the difference later. He goes on to explain a research tangle and an uppity undergrad and the three hours he spent arguing with his advisor about dead Greeks and their literal and figurative beards. But I'll give Orin this: hearing him talk about his problems has never made me jealous. He's not using the false modesty of actors and dancers trying to empathize with me by minimizing their success. He's in a different field. I'm not working against him. I never have. In all our years gaming together we've never had cross-purposes, and that's bled over to now. He may be making mountains out of my molehills, but he has my back, and I can trust him.

Once again, I am a superlative idiot.

PLAYER HARASSMENT PART 2 OF SERIOUSLY

Orin here, with the unfortunate sequel to my last post. For those who have no desire to dive into that cesspit, the fate of Duchess

Fatiguee of Altestis, *Eternal Reign* contest winner, has prompted a discussion of precisely what it means to play in an MMO with predominantly player-created content and little modly oversight. By "prompted a discussion," I mean that the resultant threads are about ten percent constructive, ten percent concern trolling, forty percent *actual* trolling, and forty percent me banning said trolls, but that's the internet for you.

In what is fast becoming a pattern, Duchess Fatiguee was approached by SummerStorm staff, to address the inactivity on her account since the coup or face revocation of her award. Leaving aside that that move is patently unfair, Fatiguee informed them of the harassment described in the post I linked above and how it made it impossible to spend time in-game doing anything but screencapping and deleting posts.

The staff member responded with this shining example of unprofessionalism.

I approached a different staff member, an active gerent (*ER* lingo for mod NPC), and asked, in light of this experience, if they would permit our characters to take political asylum on another server so that we could play unmolested. The gerent said in summary that if he afforded us this privilege, he'd have to do the same for any player who asked, including the players harassing Fatiguee. His email is capped here.

Never once did this gerent consider banning or censuring the harassers. It seems it is on Fatiguee to either endure or fold. There is no third option.

Let's continue our discussion from the previous Aqueabilitas post with a mind to this change. If the mods will not step in to reprimand egregious player behavior, what choice do we have but to comply? And in that case, what's the point of playing at all if you're not using the system to hurt other players? Once hurting players as opposed to characters becomes sanctioned, the game community ceases to be a civilized society.

The gaming industry has spent so much time trying to define itself as a form of escapism that it's become a cliché. We insist that games don't encourage violence in the real world, and that players can distinguish between fiction and reality. Every time we steal a relic or destroy a planet or enact our most lurid fantasies in digital space, we rationalize it by asserting that it harms no one. The characters in games are not real, ergo it's not really murder or rape or thievery. Gaming is a safe place to explore our darker impulses because in not harming others we allow a cathartic release of otherwise reprehensible behavior. And we rationalize and insist because we don't want our toys taken away. That's what it comes down to: people fear that if video games become subject to regulation, we will lose an outlet for our creative and, yes, destructive impulses. So by that logic, any regulation whatsoever is anathema to gaming itself.

This is *blatantly fucking false* when you commit violence against another person. Are laws about assault and rape contrary to freedom? No. You have a legal right to not get hit. You have a legal right to refuse contact with another person. You have a right to hold on to your property and expect it to remain within your control. And if one of those rights is violated, you have the right to appeal to a higher authority to enforce that right or enact restitution on your behalf. Do laws like this diminish our freedom? No. They encourage it. These restrictions allow people to pursue productive and happy ends. In the real world there are still plenty of outlets for those violent, jealous impulses that don't hurt other human beings. Go to a gun range. Talk politics on Facebook. Watch porn. *Play video games.* And in those games, if you commit a real-world crime that actually affects another human being you should be subject to real-world scrutiny and real-world punishment.

I have a feeling some of Fatiguee's trolls are going to read this. Certainly most of you will disagree with these assertions. You'll bring up slippery slopes, you'll claim that you're not harming Fatiguee's player, and you'll renounce any liability whatsoever. Since I'm fully aware of that, we can skip all those parts, and I will say this:

You deserve scrutiny. You deserve retribution. And in a civilized world, you will get it.

Comments (3004)

Okay, I can skip the first part of the thread. I know exactly what's there and every other word is *Banned*. There's much more important stuff halfway down:

O Laura O
If you do choose to take the path of political asylum, you're both welcome in our waters. If the mods won't copy your characters over for you, feel free to make clones, and I'll pull a few strings among my counts to allow you to amass some of your levels and holdings in peace. You wouldn't have your ranks, not at first, but you could keep your story going.

I wouldn't be able to have both Fatiguee and Bannedict active on that server if I took that offer, and honestly I'm inclined to forget the whole fracas at this point. But I can't get out of GeeKon because of the other Musketqueers, and I can't get out of the Fatiguee situation because of Orin's investment—which I *didn't sanction in the first place,* or the second place, but clearly it was important to him to share Publicity's email to make his point. Regardless. It's done, whether I wanted it done or not, and now I have to deal with it.

> **Orin**
> Thank you. I'll ask Fatiguee about it, since I go where she goes, but if she chooses not to go, I will proudly stay and fight. At the very least, it gets my point across to the gerents if we stand our ground.

> **O Laura O**
> If nothing else, that sets a precedent. Take good notes. Whatever happens, you're welcome on my server. Are you coming to GeeKon? If you are, I want you on my panel.

Oh fuck she's *flirting* with him.
Wait. I shouldn't assume. She was just as nice to Bannedict. Daphnis. Me. Whichever. Either way, there's other shit to do. Better

things to read than people speaking for me, and superlative humans being more in-tune with my whatever-Orin-is.

Like SummerStorm's official response to this drama, linked multiple times, four threads down:

IN REFERENCE to recent discussions on The Escapist, Aqueabilitas, Kotaku, and Twitter, we have launched an investigation into the email received by Duchess Fatiguee pertaining to her victory in the Novelization Contest. The email is not falsified, but it was not sent by our head of publicity, Mal Harding: the intern responsible has since been fired. We at SummerStorm apologize to Fatiguee on Mal's behalf. Her victory will not be rescinded on the grounds of lack of participation, and she is still scheduled to meet with SummerStorm staff at GeeKon next month.

AS WITH the previous dispute over respawn points, we make no promises about amending the gameplay, but have taken the wishes of our user base into account. This is a complicated issue, but ER is an organic system. Please bear with us as we watch the situation develop and act accordingly, when the time is right and the path is clear.

Luis Lender, aka. **Veep 2**

Good news, bad news, ugly news. All the same news. They've confirmed they're doing nothing, at least not yet. The devil you know beats the devil you don't, so that's not so awful.

But everybody knows it. Everybody paying attention to this so-called controversy now *knows* they can keep spamming my account and ostensibly no one gets hurt.

There were over five thousand messages in Fatiguee's inbox this afternoon when I burned off a chunk of my hair.

Now, there are thirty thousand.

CHAPTER SEVEN

S ir Bannedict, navigator attaché to Count Rynek, has generally escaped outside notice. His function, to chart the uncharted, masks great experience beyond his combat level, and as such he's made himself useful to the count and his fleet. The drama of Altestis has not crossed into these waters, thank fuck, and so Bannedict's job, when not grinding, consists mostly of coursing patrol routes and detecting pirate entry points so we can report them to Duchess Uhruu. It's a whole lot of jargon if I put it that way, but it amounts to fetch quests and short courier runs while I have Bannedict dip his toes in this pixilated ocean.

It's a world better than both of the others I'm living in, I'll give him that. Endless ocean. Idyllic, brightly colored banners and the glittering trappings of alien wealth. Occasional romps through the purple kelp. Knockoff Boccherini playing, like some vaguely deranged *Master and Commander* parody. What I wouldn't give to be Russell Crowe right about now. On a boat. In the middle of nowhere. Scripted. Where my actions have visible results that I can mostly control and every communiqué comes with an Accept button.

Like this one.

NEW MESSAGE: Duchess Uhruu summons you. [Text] [Voice] [Video]

Voice, I think—and then, no. No, not yet. I'm not sure how well I can manage us talking together, and Daphnis and I don't sound the same. Or look the same. Or have the same equipment, and I don't mean PC. Text it is.

UHRUU*D*: *How goes the battle?*

BANNEDICT: *the grind really. one level at a time*

UHRUU*D*: *I get that. IIRC Rynek has a raid scheduled for Wednesday. You in?*

BANNEDICT: *as far as i know*

UHRUU*D*: *Good. Advance warning: you'll probably run into a couple of the people on my watchlist. Career tributes, if you will.*

BANNEDICT: *thanks for the warning*

BANNEDICT: *i'll lay low*

UHRUU*D*: *Good. Everything else okay?*

BANNEDICT: *not not okay*

UHRUU*D*: *Ha, I get it. Anything I can help with?*

BANNEDICT: *just the whole dogpile thing*

BANNEDICT: *it's hard to watch*

UHRUU*D*: *After what you've been through? Hell yeah. And you know Orin too, so that must make it harder. It always sucks to see a friend go through this and feel like nothing you do will help.*

BANNEDICT: *amen*

UHRUU*D*: *How long have you known him?*

BANNEDICT: *seven years online*

BANNEDICT: *three offline*

UHRUU*D*: *He's not your gay roommate, is he? Did I assume wrong, that he's straight?*

BANNEDICT: *oh. no he's not alain*

BANNEDICT: *and yeah he's straight*

BANNEDICT: *that's part of the problem*

UHRUU*D*: *Problem?*

BANNEDICT: *well with how he's handling it*

BANNEDICT: *he tries but there's a lot he doesn't get, which is a pattern with him come to think of it*

BANNEDICT: *i'm sorry if this is getting too personal*

UHRUU*D*: *It's okay with me, but don't feel like you have to tell me everything. Or anything.*

BANNEDICT: *it's fine*

BANNEDICT: *and i don't want to complain about him, there's just something*

BANNEDICT: *he's like an elephant in a porcelain factory*

BANNEDICT: *i don't know how to say it in english*

UHRUU*D*: *A bull in a china shop?*

BANNEDICT: *ha cool*

BANNEDICT: *but i think elephant is more appropriate for orin*

BANNEDICT: *then again i don't know any bulls*

UHRUU*D*: *Just a lot of bullshit.*

BANNEDICT: *exactly*

BANNEDICT: *anyway, orin and i go back pretty far, like i said, and he's always been a white knight*

BANNEDICT: *the first game we played in together there was a girl playing. she must have been about fourteen but we didn't find that out until later*

BANNEDICT: *she'd lied to sign up*

BANNEDICT: *so some assholes stalked her and showed up at her high school to prove she was lying about her age*

BANNEDICT: *which is definitely a crime but they posted the photos they took anonymously so there wasn't a trail*

BANNEDICT: *orin wrote editorials and screeds until the police basically told him to shut up*

BANNEDICT: *meanwhile the girl still had to go to the same school knowing that a stranger had taken photos of her and put them on the internet*

UHRUU*D*: *Jesus.*

BANNEDICT: *it's not that he wasn't right to fight, it's just that it wasn't his fight*

BANNEDICT: *i have no idea where that girl is now*

BANNEDICT: *i hope she's okay*

BANNEDICT: *sorry*

BANNEDICT: *old drama is old*

BANNEDICT: *and in a way the fight became about something else so it's water under the bridge now*

BANNEDICT: *he means well*

UHRUU*D*: *But he knows not what he does.*

BANNEDICT: *he's better now*

BANNEDICT: *we both are*

BANNEDICT: *i won't lie, i was there too, and i definitely boosted that signal*

BANNEDICT: *not to mention, leaving that game*

UHRUU*D*: *If people only fought for the things that affected them directly, we'd be living a Randian nightmare.*

BANNEDICT: *yes*

BANNEDICT: *but is it still the same fight when someone else's voice gets louder than the victim's?*

UHRUU*D*: *I get the feeling there's a different answer to that question in France than there is in America.*

BANNEDICT: *is there really?*

BANNEDICT: *wow this is getting heavy*

UHRUU*D*: *As long as Fatiguee isn't fighting, it's going to be hard for her to determine the course of the fight. I hate to say it, but until she speaks up, no one can take her opinion into account. And Orin seems to know what she wants, even if she hasn't gone public with it, so if she trusts him, the rest of us have to.*

BANNEDICT: *right*

UHRUU*D*: *Do you know Fatiguee too?*

BANNEDICT: *only in passing*

BANNEDICT: *otherwise just orin*

BANNEDICT: *i've never met fatiguee in person*

UHRUU*D*: *Do you mind if I ask what he's like?*

BANNEDICT: *he's basically the same as he is online*

BANNEDICT: *that was one of the first things i noticed*

BANNEDICT: *i didn't have a picture and i still recognized him*

UHRUU*D*: *Sounds like the start of a story.*

BANNEDICT: *well he guessed that i was me too without a picture*

BANNEDICT: *it probably helped that i have an accent*

UHRUU*D*: *And a headshot with your stats writ large at the bottom.*

BANNEDICT: *shit my headshot is so out of date*

BANNEDICT: *i have copies in black and white with the same photo*

BANNEDICT: *thanks for reminding me*

UHRUU*D*: *Ha, anytime.*

BANNEDICT: *but if you mean am i distinctive looking? i'd have to think about that*

BANNEDICT: *i mean you know what it's like having to see yourself how other people see you? knowing what your colors are? your selling points? your weight minus ten and your height plus two?*

UHRUU*D*: *Ha! I always got told to leave the weight column blank. Or put something "sassy" in it.*

BANNEDICT: *for fucks sake*

UHRUU*D*: *But I do know what you mean. It's one of the reasons I got out. I already have to deal with How They See Me enough. I didn't want to make a career of it. You probably have much thicker skin than I do.*

BANNEDICT: *i definitely don't. i just pick different fights i guess*

BANNEDICT: *it helps that i don't have to fight as hard as my friends*

BANNEDICT: *i mean, take the gay fight for instance*

BANNEDICT: *i didn't fight it, i just told people for years that my orientation was shrug*
or fuck-deficit

UHRUU*D*: *You're bi?*

BANNEDICT: *pan's closer but honestly i've never cared about anatomy. i worry too much about my own to spare a fuck for anyone else's. not that it matters much these days*

UHRUU*D*: *I feel you. Between law school and my online commitments I haven't had time either.*

BANNEDICT: *your excuse is better than mine*

BANNEDICT: *i'm just out of work*

UHRUU*D*: *No, there are plenty of fish in this sea. Civil Rights Law is a lesbian magnet.*

BANNEDICT: *you're gay?*

UHRUU*D*: *Bi. But admitting an attraction to men doesn't mean I want a relationship with one. There's a whole conversation about practice and inclination that I can copy and paste into this window if you're interested.*

Interested. What a loaded word.

BANNEDICT: *don't you hate having to do that*

BANNEDICT: *i mean explain everything. have it packaged up and ready to copy and paste*

BANNEDICT: *i know i do*

UHRUU*D*: *Sometimes. But getting it out there's more important to me. So other people have a way to explain how they feel, if they're struggling like I was growing up.*

BANNEDICT: *see i get that. but what if it didn't have to be explained at all*

BANNEDICT: *what if people could just let what they are inside go unsaid, and what if you don't want to label it in the first place*

UHRUU*D*: *Then you don't have to.*

BANNEDICT: *but then other people do it for you*

BANNEDICT: *what if your decision is not to decide?*

UHRUU*D*: *Well, I suppose you could leave them a clue. A shoe, perhaps. And then see what they'll do.*

UHRUU*D*: *If you catch my meaning.*

BANNEDICT: *oh god I got sondheim all over this conversation*

BANNEDICT: *phone rings, door chimes, in comes fuckery*

UHRUU*D*: *Ha!*

BANNEDICT: *i guess i'm just sick of casting notices deciding what i am*

BANNEDICT: *sick of having a type*

BANNEDICT: *being a type*

BANNEDICT: *directors look at you and don't see who you are*

BANNEDICT: *they see how well you match up to what they think you are*

BANNEDICT: *how well you fit into their available slot*

BANNEDICT: *and either you file yourself down to fit it but then what's left and how much of it is you*

BANNEDICT: *or you opt out and get nothing anyway*

BANNEDICT: *because there aren't any roles for the person you want to be*

BANNEDICT: *the one you are on the inside*

BANNEDICT: *for all that the theater is for moving beyond your body the world still defines you by it*

BANNEDICT: *by what you were born with and grow into*

BANNEDICT: *it's why I got out of classical dance*

BANNEDICT: *where the women are delicate sylphides and the men are strapping knights and there's no space in between for people who aren't either*

BANNEDICT: *who don't want to be either*

BANNEDICT: *taglioni got up on pointe and all of a sudden dance meant one thing to women and another thing to men and there's no way to just dance*

BANNEDICT: *just like there's no way to just act*

BANNEDICT: *you're an actor or an actress*

BANNEDICT: *not a person who acts*

BANNEDICT: *and it's so fucking important what chromosomes you've got that even in a world that claims to let you be anything you want, you still have to be what they say you are first*

BANNEDICT: *a man*

BANNEDICT: *or a woman*

BANNEDICT: *only two options on the casting list*

UHRUU*D*: *I get the feeling this isn't just about casting.*

BANNEDICT: *well no*

BANNEDICT: *but that's an even heavier conversation that i won't subject anyone to, let alone you*

UHRUU*D*: *That's fair, and entirely your prerogative.*

BANNEDICT: *thanks*

BANNEDICT: *are you angry with me?*

UHRUU*D*: *Not at all. But do you mind if I do something more than listen?*

BANNEDICT: *depends on what it is*

UHRUU*D*: *I have a last name that's an immediate signal that I'm not white. So when I was trying to break through in LA, I had two headshot/resume combos; one with my legal name, and one with my stage name, which was deliberately ethnically ambiguous. Honestly, I got more callbacks with my real name, but for worse parts, and I even caught myself acting differently at the auditions when people called me Laura Hanson instead of Laura Oweyo. Because I thought they were looking for someone whiter, I'd try to be it. Which is disgusting, so I stopped doing it. People can't just turn off their eyes and filter out something I can't change, and more to the point don't want to, and shouldn't have to.*

UHRUU*D*: *Wall of text, sorry.*

BANNEDICT: *justified wall of text*

BANNEDICT: *compared to mine before that's barely a fence*

BANNEDICT: *and i'm sorry*

BANNEDICT: *but i guess the question is whether the parts I don't want them to see are things I can change, or shouldn't have to*

UHRUU*D*: *Honestly? I think you're awesome just the way you are, and if I were a director I'd find some place to cast you.*

BANNEDICT: *but what if this isn't who i am*
UHRUU*D*: *I don't know, ask Jean Valjean.*
BANNEDICT: *fffffff*
BANNEDICT: *what*
BANNEDICT: *sorry*
BANNEDICT: *actually laughing so hard i woke one of my roommates*
UHRUU*D*: *Mission accomplished.*

What a loaded conversation.

The excellent thing about mindless grinding—the not-so-fun kind of mindless grinding, alas—is that it frees up a great deal of auxiliary brain space for analyzing ethics and identity. That same space may also be occupied by spiders and abject terror, of course, but the point is that there's extra space, and like most vacuums, my nature abhors it.

That was quite possibly the most liberating conversation I have ever had. And almost every word of it was true. The only thing I actually lied about was that I've never met Fatiguee, and even that isn't a lie really. After all, as Orin would probably put in superlative dissertation bullshit, can one truly know oneself? Can it not be said that due to the nature of time and consciousness, that no person is capable of comprehending the intricacies of Self? What is Self? What is what? What is a man but a miserable pile of secrets?

But enough talk. Have at me.

Am I a man? No. But does that make me a woman? Or am I just frustrated with people telling me what a woman is?

Well, I'm clearly frustrated about *something*. I'm also clearly confused about a whole lot of other shit, so maybe it's all bleeding over. How much of me being a woman is directors? How much is *assigned*? I've certainly played male roles in workshops and readings, and when there just weren't enough men available, and it didn't matter a lick. Plus I got to kiss girls, which is awesome. And yes, I've been more interested in male roles in practically every show I've auditioned for, but that's because female roles in my age group tend to suck.

The possibility that really turns my stomach is that I'm as brainwashed as all those directors. I don't even know how long I've been steeped in *gender*. It's easy enough to say I don't look at it in other people, not as potential hookups anyway, but how long have I been defining myself as a woman just because other people do? Do I have the right to decide that I'm fed up with being a woman and don't want a part of this bullshit when there are people out there who feel decisively male no matter what skin they're in? And it's not that being male is having a male body, obviously, but how much of this gender conundrum is good old-fashioned penis envy? I could dismiss myself in a heartbeat: *you're not trans, you're just frustrated being a girl because you have to work harder. You don't want to be a man, you just want all the perks. You want to have your cock and eat it too.*

Which opens up a new question: what do I *do* about it? If anything. Because why start now? I've done nothing about it yet. Then again, doing nothing isn't working.

Neither is grinding. The fish aren't biting. Semiliterally.

I pry myself off the computer, log out, and check under the door. It's five in the morning—Jackie's not up yet, and as far as I know Alain's just gotten to sleep, so I shouldn't wake him. Looks like I'm wrestling these demons alone, then. That's not so bad. I can do that. This kind of inner demon doesn't even tap at my hit points.

Maybe the decision is best made after some sleep. I think I slept last night. Or this morning. Well, *now* is this morning. I lie down on top of the covers but something in the mattress (and my mind) doesn't quite sink. Am I wrong about who I am? And do I have to start quoting *Les Misérables* or will that happen on its own?

Can I picture myself as a man? That's basically Bannedict. Or Daphnis. Like myself, but male. Maybe a little harder in the face. Maybe a haircut that doesn't require me to do my roots all the time. Bigger feet. A flat chest—not that that's much of a stretch. A dick. Would that feel strange? I've never packed to pass: dick silhouette doesn't matter as much onstage. I should ask Jackie about it later. But right now the thought isn't completely abhorrent. Or abhorrent at all, really. I like vaginas, and I definitely don't mind my own. But would it feel different to have something on the outside?

It's still not right. But in this imperfect world, the only way to be seen as not-a-woman is to be decisively a man.

Okay. I should make a list. Because items five, four, three, and two of this impending gender-crisis itinerary are all fighting to be the one to make it through.

Five: I am mentally okay with the possibility that I might be trans. Or at least not cis. Or whatever.

Four: I am mentally okay with the idea of further self-scrutiny and experimentation. It's not like I have anything else to do, and I've technically been doing that online already. And there *is* GeeKon. Cons are full of people I've never seen and will never see again, and they're safer spaces than the real world by far, and I *definitely* wouldn't be the first whose badge didn't match his ID.

Three: I am not not-okay with trying this out in meatspace. The prospect still seems dishonest, and a more pertinent kind of dishonest than what I'm doing in *Eternal Reign*. Bannedict is only an alt. Daphnis might not be.

Two: I could meet Laura. As the version of myself she knows.

Then I guess One is: My life's already a garbage fire. I might as well dance in the flames.

Alain comes back from a run at about nine thirty in the morning. I've already taken his spot on the couch. It's mine. He can't ignore it.

He smiles through his sweat. "You want to take a turn on co-op?"

"I want you to make me into a dude," I say.

Alain throws the keys clear across the room and tackles me to the couch like he won the lottery.

CHAPTER EIGHT

Having a career drag queen design your male persona is like asking a celebrity pastry chef to make you a chili dog.

"So let me get this straight," Alain says, throwing a bundle of T-shirts in my face as he rummages through his dresser. "You want to spend GeeKon as a man?"

"Sort of." I start folding the shirts, since they were never folded to begin with, which gives me an excuse to look at the ostentatious insanity he wants me to wear. T-shirts, sure: T-shirts with two-toned sequin gashes that make it look like I bleed glitter, no. "So I've been playing a male alt, and some people assumed I was a male player."

"And they're assuming Fatiguee is female," Alain guesses, right off the bat.

"Yeah." There's no point in hiding it. "Plus, you know—I'm starting to think it might be true. That I might like being a guy."

Something jangles, and Alain blinks down at me over the waistband of a pair of leather-and-chain pants that will never, ever fit me. "Might like, or might be?"

"Still don't know," I admit, "but I'm not doing so great as myself lately. Might as well try being someone else."

"It doesn't work that way," Jackie says, leaning on the doorjamb. I'm not sure if she plans on going out today, but she's mostly dressed—no pants and no shoes, but everything else. We might have interrupted her getting ready for something, shit. "Are you trying to be someone else, or are you trying to figure yourself out?"

Alain shuts the dresser drawer and turns to perch on it. "She's right. And that choice makes a huge difference in how we can help you."

"It's fine, you don't have to—"

A hand comes down on my shoulder: Jackie's. "We are. Deal with it."

"So." Alain taps his heels against the drawers. "Who is this guy you plan on being?"

Somehow, hearing it framed that way makes it easier. "The backstory I gave her was basically the same as my own. He's an actor and a gamer. More confident than me."

Alain grins, and doesn't laugh *too* much. "I hope he has better fashion sense than you, otherwise I've got nothing to work with."

"I don't want to look like I'm cosplaying. I want Daphnis to feel real. Like I've always been him."

"Okay, so we're going for a no-makeup transformation. You want to look like you woke up as someone else and could just go about your business, and you want to pass."

I nod.

"See, that's a problem, because you have *zero aesthetic*," he teases, and I know it's teasing but still, that's the last thing I want to hear.

"What would you do differently if you weren't female?" Jackie asks.

"Not worry about burning off my hair."

They both laugh this time, Alain more than Jackie of course. "Well, that's an easy fix. How edgy can your haircut get before you piss off your agent?"

I look Alain in the eyes like I'm staring down a float of weresharks. "Until my agent sends me a role I can work with, he gets no say in *anything*."

"Great! Jackie, set up the kitchen! It's Hair Day X-2!"

For once, the sequel turns out to be much better overall than the original. After the towels are out of the laundry I still haven't done and spread on the floor, Alain sits me down in a chair and gets to work. He carefully shaves the burned side of my head, and the other to match, then starts trimming the Mohawk until it's fuzzy-short in the back and longer the closer it gets to my forehead. He goes on about how he's always wanted to do something like this to his own hair but not enough to thin it, and I'm content to play mannequin until he decides he's done. Somehow, with less of it, the parts I can see feel wispier, more silvery than they were in that uneven dye job.

"I want to dye the tips!" he croons before I even get a proper view, but hey. "What color *don't* you want it to be?"

"Orange."

"Great, I'll do teal."

"The scar shows," Jackie points out from the couch. She picked the anime again. This time the schoolgirls aren't lesbians, but they're taking off their clothes at every available opportunity anyway. What the fuck is the plot of this show?

Never mind. I touch the side of my head. It's still sore and blistered, but yeah, it feels kind of tough. Literally and symbolically.

"Exactly," Alain says. "People will see that before they look at your chin. And it shows you don't care. Scars equal badass, especially head scars."

"Badass doesn't mean masculine," Jackie corrects from the couch.

"No, but we can't all be Imperator Furiosa. It's about the *contrast*. If you want to compensate for natural femininity, you have to be more masculine than you mean to be. It takes extra force to change directions."

"Yes," Jackie winces, "but there aren't only two directions."

"It's fine," I cut in before this gets too heated—or before Alain pulls what little remains of my hair out while he's pinching the ends with dye. "I want to look stronger. Like I can take a hit."

Alain leans over me, like he's going to give me a Spider-Man kiss, but he just preens. "Now *that's* something I can work with. What are some of your diva—I mean hero inspirations? Try to stick to ones I know."

I try to recall the stuff we've all watched or played together. There are plenty of people who look like I want Daphnis to look, now that I think about it: tough but not imposing. A survivor, stronger than he lets on. Someone who doesn't cave under pressure, unlike certain other people in my life—namely me. Someone who can make people see what he sees.

"William Thatcher from *A Knight's Tale*," I say. "Or Spike Spiegel. Or, um, that guy with the spiky blond hair and the sword that's bigger than him."

"Cloud Strife." Alain blinks. "That's edgier than I thought you'd go."

"If you plan on covering me in belts I will end this *right now*."

"A hidden prince," Jackie says, from where she's otherwise glued to the television screen. "Make her a damn *oujisama*, you know what they're like."

"I'm not a prince," I say.

"But that's what you're describing."

"I'll settle for duke." I'm only half-joking. God, I'd love to sic Bannedict on Krozin's ass and dismantle this ridiculous coup. But Bannedict's on Laura's server, not mine.

"Not a hidden prince, an Iron Woobie." Alain circles me in the chair, uncannily like a Bond villain about to commence an interrogation. Javier Bardem should sue. Oh—Javier Bardem. I could pass for a young Javier Bardem. "There's a theme there. Disheveled but not destroyed. No—indestructible."

In the end, Daphnis could pass for a couple of years younger than me. Like the fraternal twin version of me, like Jaime would have been to Cersei when they were teenagers, creepy as that thought is. Tousled bleached-and-green hair in a loose Mohawk. No makeup. Worse posture. Lifts in the boots. One of Jackie's harnesses and packers. The most boyfriend pair of jeans I own, since none of Alain's fit me, and two tank tops: one tight and black (Jackie's binder), one loose and gray (Alain's gym shirt). My three sabers tattoo is on display on my biceps, which appears more toned in the tank tops for some reason. Only one belt (that was a fight), and only one cuff, a black leather number with a wolf-mounted D-ring that one of Alain's kinkier exes got him years ago. And a navy hooded *Saltwater Sandbox* sweatshirt, because if I'm going to a con in this I have to fly the official colors for *Eternal Reign*.

Daphnis looks like he walked off the set of *Stage Beauty* or *Shakespeare in Love*. Daphnis looks like all the boys I envied so much when I got bit parts in every play and wanted their songs, their roles, their voices. Daphnis looks like he could succeed wherever I've failed.

I fiddle with his bangs, and they're mine. It doesn't keep the tears out of my eyes, but does stop them from falling.

Alain lays out a vaguely Elizabethan-fantasy costume for me to wear to the con, apparently, when I'm not in street clothes, that's right out of the promotional art. Jerkin and codpiece and cloak. Too big, he says, but, "There's time."

Funny: it feels *true*.

Funny, but I'm crying anyway.

CHAPTER NINE

Richard Gere is doing a perverse fan dance in my dreams. There's an awful lot of glitter, and his voice is nasal as hell. And tinny. I don't remember the sound mixing being this awful in *Chicago*.

Chicago.

Oh fuck my life, it's my agent on the phone. Time to get up now.

"*Bonjour?*"

"English, Daphne."

"Morning, Julio. Is this too big for email?"

"It wasn't yesterday when I emailed you about it. It is now that you have two hours to get down to Ripley-Grier if you want a chance."

"Sorry, I was away yesterday," I lie, though it's not a complete lie since I spent yesterday becoming someone else and avoiding the internet. "What show is this for?"

"National tour of *An American in Paris* just lost its understudy for Lise. The details are in the email, but they've already got your package, so they know what to expect. I assume you can be there by ten."

I roll out of bed enough to check the laptop clock. It's five after eight, and I look nothing like my headshot.

I put as much pep into my voice as I can. "What choice do I have?"

I'll say this for the short hair: it makes getting out the door easier.

I read the email while brushing my teeth: they want me dance-ready first. After they see that I can dance, they'll want singing and sides. I bust out the lucky leotard and throw Alain's tank top over it. They'll want to see my legs but not until I get there, so yoga pants.

I haven't unpacked my kit bag since the last audition, so everything is still in it, which means it all smells faintly of undone laundry and pencil shavings, but there's nothing I can do about that, ergo I don't. The bodega provides a PowerBar-and-water breakfast. I spend most of the subway ride down holding on to the pole and stretching out my calves and neck.

It serves me right for gaming all night after being made over all day, but at least now I can say that I'm chasing that elusive dream, that I'm doing what I came back to New York for. Which is more than I *could* say.

Ripley-Grier Studios welcomes me with an apathetic doorman and only two elevators' worth of a queue, which gives me enough time to check my face. No zits. Freckles behaving. Under-eye bags, but nothing that concealer can't handle. One of my eyebrows dried frizzy, but sweat will take care of that, I think. No time for eyeliner but mascara will do. I don't have enough time to slap lipstick concealer on my tattoo, so thank god for that bandana.

When I finally get into the elevator, I can't help taking inventory. The really hot Korean lady in the low-cut red dress gets off on the tenth floor, black binder in hand. Opera, most likely. Not competition. Two brunettes who look like they stepped out of a Fitbit ad get off on my floor but head down the opposite hall. One taller, thinner, obvious ballerina is two steps ahead of me right up to the audition door.

The manager screens her first. Her name is Chantilly. I wish I were making that up.

"Checking in?" the manager asks me, once she's three-quarters of the way through eyeing me up and down.

"Yes—Daphne Benoit."

She raises an eyebrow, but makes the check on her clipboard. "Go on in and stretch. We should start in five minutes."

If I don't initiate my smile protocols, I'll forget in five minutes. So I force the teeth like a pageant queen and walk on in.

I am one of ten. The other eight, plus Chantilly, have immediate similarities. They're as pristine and uniform as Rockettes, even the ones who are shorter than me: flattering-colored sports bras with the correct amount of jiggle, hair back in ponytails to show off the malleable length, sufficient makeup to sweat through. There's no one I recognize from any of the other shows I've done, but that's happened before. They're in pairs or solo, stretching or going through forms, pretending not to notice the table of men in the corner with scorecards and folders and two cups of coffee each. The girls see me, though. They see me because that's what we *do* to each other.

Some stare. I keep smiling, set down my bag, and pretend not to notice, just like them.

The floor-to-ceiling mirror doubles us all. I don't look like myself in it, and I don't look like I belong in this line, but fuck it. I can use that. I can be a guaranteed standout. What Would Daphnis Do? Well, Daphnis wouldn't be auditioning for the ingénue role in *An American in Paris*, he'd be gunning for the lead, and he'd get it because he wouldn't let them say no.

The assistant director calls the roll. I'm Daphne, not Daphnis.

The dance combination takes ten minutes to learn, and the choreographer only talks to our reflections. He drops words like *delicate* and *graceful* and *classic*, tells us to mind our hands so we don't accidentally evoke *Cats*. We all laugh on cue to prove we get the joke, and sneak glances at the casting table. I catch on quickly enough, faster than some. Chantilly isn't that quick, actually. Graceful, yes, but slow on the uptake. I can do this. I am doing this. I've got a leotard full of sweat that says I'm doing this.

"First round of cuts," the choreographer says. He rattles off four names, and none of them are mine. They go, with thanks. I stay. So does this permanent smile protocol. "The rest of you, take five, then we'll see you individually in alphabetical order. Daphne, you're first, so don't go far."

I don't go far. I barely go anywhere. I don't even towel off, just sit on a bench in the hall while the same thing goes on in every other room on every other floor. I was one of ten. Now I'm one of six. I'm not the shortest or the tallest. I'm probably the heaviest and the flattest but that could be what they want, since they cut the others. And those remaining have hair in natural colors and symmetrical cuts, even if some are highlighted and some are between dye jobs, but it's hair. Hair is malleable. Maybe I should have borrowed one of Alain's wigs on the way out the door. Maybe that would help them see what they want.

Five minutes pass, then six. I want to go off and use the bathroom, but then I might miss my call. Better to hold it and wait. Seven minutes. I run through the combination in my head, practice the *delicate graceful classic* hand gestures the choreographer wants, take off the tank top so I can get some of the sweat off my neck. At eight minutes, the manager comes out into the hall and waves me in

Smile protocol. Men at a table. I can be what they want. *I am what they want, whether they know it or not.*

"*Bonjour*," I say, then, "Hello," making a point of my accent. It gets their attention, makes the AD look up from my headshot and the choreographer chuckle.

"Nice to meet you, Daphne," the director says, glancing down at my file. "Almost didn't recognize you." Before I can say anything to that, he goes on, "Settle something for me: is it *Ben-owit* or *Ben-wa?*"

"*Ben-wa*," I answer, careful not to make fun of his pronunciation or offer any jokes. Just smile. *Just smile, and do what they say, and be what they want, and maybe they'll like you.*

"Told you," the choreographer tells the director, then turns to me. "Is your family French?"

"Yes, I was born there." I have a whole script prepared for this line of questioning. I worked it out with my agent in advance. "I've only lived here since high school."

"Ah, the genuine article." The director grins—it's not quite a leer, he's probably too swishy for that—and waves at the pianist. "Let's start with the combination."

From there, it is, literally, the same old song and dance. I know I don't mess up: I keep concentrating on my hands. Graceful. Delicate. Classic.

"That was lovely," the AD says, "but could you be a skosh more feminine?"

I will not say, *Feminine how?* I will not say, *Feminine how?* I will not say, *Feminine how?*

"All right." I smile, brightly but (I hope) softly, and nod at the pianist when I'm ready to do it again.

I dance the same steps. I relax my face, slow my gestures, try not to stick out my chin. There is only so much I can do about my body when I'm using it like this, but they want *feminine*, and that's Alain's version of feminine, like my character shoes are five-inch heels. Like I'm missing a partner and dancing in the passive voice.

"Better," the AD nods, and the director makes a few notes, and whoever the other man is thumbs at my résumé with his eyebrow in a perfect Pixar curve.

They make it clear that it's time for me to sing. I bring my binder to the pianist, talk over the tempo with him, and try not to listen over my shoulder. The panel is whispering, just low enough and English enough that I can't eavesdrop without straining. And I shouldn't. I already know what they're saying.

They expected one thing. They got something else.

I sing my thirty-two bars of Gershwin. "Someone to Watch Over Me." It's exactly what they asked for, exactly what Lise sings, like Kay before her in *Oh, Kay!*, because they're basically the same role. I give the panel the vulnerability they claim to crave, and whoever I'm singing to is accordingly not the man some girls think of as handsome, but he's a man, and that's all I want really, because that's all any ingénue wants, ever. I let the men at the table think I need them. I do need them. I need them much more than they need me. They could find another me on the street. A better me. Delicate, graceful, classic. Feminine.

"Thank you for coming, Daphne," the AD says. "We'll call you."

No, you won't.

CHAPTER TEN

NEW MESSAGE: Duchess Uhruu summons you. [Text] [Voice] [Video]

Well, a word from the duchess is definitely a reason to pause in my continued quest for purple kelp. I might be overfishing. I hover my mouse over the [Text] hail, and then. Wait.

Maybe not.

"Alain? Jackie?" I call into the living room. Jackie's pulling her shoes on, and Alain's zipping tonight's drag outfit into a bag. "Do I pass?"

Jackie leans in from the couch, raises an eyebrow. "You look fine."

"You'd better," Alain laughs. "What, you planning on going out?"

"No, video chat."

"Then you're definitely fine. She'll love it."

That's a choice endorsement. And Daphnis in the mirror has the face I want him to have, and I'm not getting anywhere sitting around the apartment farming kelp. Plus, if Daphne is dead in the figurative water and Daphnis *is* me, I'd love for Laura to be the first to meet him. Well, the first other than the Musketqueers.

I scoot the cursor over to [Video] instead, and click it before I can change my mind.

Miraculously, my heart doesn't burst out of my chest in the time it takes the window to boot up. There's lag, and it turns out her camera quality isn't amazing, but—

But what I *can* see is breathtaking.

Laura turns out to have natural hair, cut not too short, and she might be the only black girl I've ever met with such prominent freckles. She has big red glasses that match her lipstick, and she's *smiling,* and shit, I want to see that smile every day.

"Change of pace?" she asks.

"It's, um—" Wow, clearly Daphnis isn't as articulate as I am in the face of pretty girls. Um. Actually I'm not that articulate with girls either. I try again. Keep my voice low. "It's hard to—" Nope, one more time! "I was curious. If it would work." If *I* would work. Which it seems like I am.

"Your accent is adorable." She leans in, grinning. "And so's your hair."

Do guys blush? Well, the guy version of me does, it turns out. "My roommate just did it yesterday."

"The dye?"

"Yeah." The cut too, but she doesn't have to know that.

"Alain's got great taste." She even pronounces his name correctly. This is definitely too good to be true. I can't help smiling, and there's no protocol about it.

And if she keeps complimenting me, I'm going to fuck this all up. "I really like your glasses."

"Thanks! I do too, but it's hell matching reds."

"It's working."

"Does your agent let you get away with the green?"

I hope that when Daphnis grimaces, it doesn't look as schooled and—ha—feminine as it tends to when I do it. "I haven't cleared it with him yet. But it's hair, it grows." And after today, I'll probably have to tell Julio, especially if word gets back to him about my not lining up with the headshot he sent out.

"And you can still get cast if you don't have any." There is something dorky as hell about the way she winks. Maybe it's the glasses. Maybe it's her round cheeks. Either way it's going straight to my heart.

She basically just said that I pass. That she sees a guy, because she sees someone who isn't bound by female strictures. It's *working*. I continue to be a lying sack of shit—maybe—but it's working.

"Actually, I had an audition today." It feels right to tell her. "I didn't get up to sides."

"That sucks." She crinkles her nose. "They're missing out."

I shrug. "I wasn't what they wanted, that's all."

"I wish it weren't about that."

"About what they wanted?"

"Yeah. And what they expect other people to want. That part's even worse in LA. It's expectations on expectations. Market trends. Algorithms. It's this self-perpetuating cycle of trope reinforcement that stifles anything resembling creativity and relegates people to specializations at the expense of innovation."

"Blog post?"

"Yeah, two years ago." She cracks up. "It compared film casting to multivariable calculus where the limit is always approaching White. I was a little heavy-handed about it."

"Well, some anvils need to be dropped."

"Oh, no. Don't get me sucked in to TV Tropes."

"Sorry!"

"It's fine, I'm kidding. I've got a Skype about the GeeKon panel coming up soon anyway, so I won't have time."

"How's panel prep going?"

She was already lit up from talking about her blog; now she's figuratively shining so much that I might have to adjust the brightness on my screen. "Not bad at all. Tonight we're delegating sections and setting up the PowerPoint. I get the feeling that most of it is going to be roundtable, and I want to be as current as possible, but there still needs to be a foundation and a framework."

"That sounds like a lot. I mean, I've never done a panel at a con before."

"It *is* a lot, but it's fun. And it becomes a Thing You Do, I guess. I have some SHMUP friends who basically have a roadshow they take from con to con and they haven't had to pay for badges or rooms in ten years."

"Seems worth it."

"It definitely is. Do you get to many cons?"

"I did in high school and college. Less now. Jackie goes to a lot, but GeeKon is going to be my first in a couple of years."

"Logistics?"

"Yeah. Either I have the time off, or I *really* don't."

She laughs, nods, grins, *gets it*. She's been there. "It'll be great to meet you—"

The text tone on my phone pings, loud enough to echo on Laura's side of the screen. Then again, and again, hiccoughing through the interface. I left my phone back on the bed, I think—yeah, there it is—and it pings again.

My intestines just tied themselves into sausage links.

"I should get that," I tell Laura, and I try not to grimace but I'm not sure I succeed.

"Go ahead—I should probably get these ops done before the panel Skype. If you want to, I'd love to talk another time."

Well, even if I was grimacing, I'm not now. "So would I."

Another text ping just as I sign off *ER*—wow, this must be a huge deal, whatever it is. Or maybe I got roped into a group text. Have I forgotten someone's birthday in France?

No. It's Orin.

I'm sorry
I'm so sorry
I didn't mean this I swear
Please believe me
I need to call you and I don't know if you're awake
So when you get this please call

I can't get to my contacts file fast enough. This is an actual emergency. Actual danger. I've never seen Orin panic, not in all these years, and if this is what it's like—

"Hey," he says. Mostly breath.

"Hey yourself," I can't help responding. "What's wrong?"

"Don't freak out— Okay, that's the worst way to get someone to not freak out, I know. I'm sorry. But. I'm calling from the Rochester precinct."

"The *police*? Orin—"

"It's for my own protection. They, um. The trolls. They've found my apartment."

I know what he's going to say before he says it.

"And they're looking for yours."

CHAPTER ELEVEN

FATIGUEE AND SACHEM — CONSPIRACY AND HYPOCRISY

SJW Orin Knecht, professional wet blanket at apologist stomping-ground Aqueabilitas and *Eternal Reign* player, likes to think he's all about fair play. He's gone on and on and on about players supposedly misusing out-of-game behaviors to cheat at *ER*, which is impossible for a game with no rules, but what the fuck ever. Turns out Orin's just as opportunistic as the rest of us; he's merely using a smokescreen.

Our anonymous investigation has turned up a shitload of evidence that Orin Knecht, aka Count Sachem, and Duchess Fatiguee, whose legal name we have yet to track down but who went by the handle MdmGuillotine for the early stages of their relationship, have been conspiring for years to undermine the players on their server. And, what's worse, they're letting their sexual relationship interfere with everyone else's enjoyment.

The saga goes back seven years. Orin and Fatiguee first met in Clan Ghoti in the heyday of *Elfhaven Online*. Here is the IRC log where they were introduced. (Note that this may have been staged, and it could go back further, but they definitely act like it's their first time. Then again, so did your whore ex-girlfriend.) That particular IRC channel was active until three years ago, and we have logs that show their collaboration across several other MMOs, including Ultimate Odyssey Online, Periapta, Dragon Strych, ZxA, and Elfhaven Legendia.

But that's just the public face of these chat logs. We have the private ones.

Three years ago, during Dragon Strych. TLDR: They arrange to meet in person at NYGC.

During NYGC. The blonde sucking Orin's face is almost definitely Fatiguee because after NYGC, they cyber like it's 1999. And it's not the only time.

Fatiguee is, apparently, a professional actress. Not surprising. Even less surprising, she started using Orin to cover for her in-game when she was ostensibly at rehearsals, as far back as *Elfhaven Legendia*. Check the dates—the cybersex continues when she's not playing. Trading text handjobs for loot? Clearly that's fair play, huh Orin?

With IRC out of the picture, and now that they're using text messages, we don't have as much amateur porn from the last year. But we do have logs from Eternal Reign, including their very first one. Which contained this exchange, emphasis mine:

FATIGUEE: Actually I've been toying with the idea of a fey court.

SACHEM: A fae court?

FATIGUEE: You know, nobles vying for power. Wheels within wheels. Using mortal pawns because they're expendable.

SACHEM: I think there's a place for that in ER. But it's going to take time.

FATIGUEE: So we'll take time. **Between the two of us we can take over the server.** And then it's court en miniature.

SACHEM: Are you sure?

FATIGUEE: Even if I can't, you can. And it will work. Whichever one of us gets ops can op the other. Like if you have grading or I have a show.

SACHEM: That does work. **And if we can't be together IRL, we'll always have this.**

Fair play, gentlemen. That's the face of fair play.

Well, sure enough, they got their wish. They took over the server. Fatiguee continues to fuck off for long periods and makes people fight over her, by her own admission according to *The Annals of Altestis* that she's so fucking proud of.

So they're both hypocrites. Fatiguee does only half the work and wants all the fame, and that's a pattern going back years. Orin claims he's all about fair play, but he's been gaming the system like all the so-called troglodytes he's banning from Aqueabilitas. But I have to give Fatiguee credit: she's not pretending to be anything but the manipulative, lying whore she is. Orin's just pathetic.

And if you want the coup de grace, we've got it. Orin is a doctoral candidate at the University of Rochester. His field of study? The philosophy of player behavior. He's written papers on all of you, and he's made money off of them. And I'll bet the IRB has a thing or two to say about the ethics of his research.

People in glass houses shouldn't throw stones, Orin. They get cut.

He's done his call to arms: so shall we. Let Orin know what we think of his hypocrisy. Call him at home, or at work. Call his dissertation advisor and tell him that his padawan is a crock of shit who's using school resources to promote a selfish agenda. Call his parents and tell them just what their son has been getting up to online with his whore. Email Aqueabilitas and get him removed from their staff. And if you don't want to call, you can always try to find him in person at 166 Tawn Ct., Apartment C, in Rochester, NY. Or track him at his classes, which are publicly accessible.

Call him until Orin apologizes for his behavior, and Fatiguee rescinds her ill-gotten victory in the ER Novelization Contest. And if she won't, it's only a matter of time before we find her too. Where an asshole goes, a cunt can't be far behind.

If there is one thing I have learned in all these years of acting, it's that: what I am never matters, only What They See.

I can't disagree with what they see. That's the worst part. Almost everything they've said about Orin is technically true. So is just about everything they've said about me. Never mind how they got the logs: we still said all those things. It's all true, the same way that $2+2=5$ for sufficiently large values of 2. The same way that the magic of theater's suspension of disbelief let's us accept people bursting into choreographed production numbers in the middle of the street.

We played together across every one of those MMOs, true. We coordinated outside of the games, true. Objectively, it's no different than the mass effort to flood my inbox: same technique. Intent doesn't mean shit if you're arguing actuality.

We hooked up at NYGC three years ago, true. That's me in the photo, with bra-length bleached-blond hair and a *Check Out My Hoard* sweatshirt, kissing Orin. The trolls don't know why. They don't care why. They have no need of nuance, of how amazingly cathartic it feels to put a face to someone who's understood you from the start, how lonely I was trying to get my life started in New York City with my family back overseas, how it felt to anchor myself to someone who seemed to have it all under control and never told me I wasn't good enough. My feelings don't matter to people who want facts.

We divided our time when I had IRL commitments, true. We had to. I was with the national tour of *Catch Me If You Can*, dancing in the chorus and covering Brenda. Eight shows a week, two cities a month, for an entire year. I was lucky if I could call my parents and tell them I hadn't been trampled by buffalo. But I can't come clean about that because then they *will* know who I am, and I'll be in the same place as Orin, only less credible a plaintiff because the police have already told me there's nothing they can do in a perpetratorless crime, and if I call again with the same problem, they'll say I'm crying wolf. So it's either let the accusations stand, or open myself to further fire, and either way the trolls win.

We really did say we were going to take over the server for a court game. And I novelized it. It was just a story. Orin and I haven't seen each other in person in three years. Not since that one weekend. So yes, the trolls can say we're enacting a fantasy of being together and forcing everyone else in on it for our own sick amusement. It's as true as it needs to be. It can be spun that way, and doesn't take much spinning.

But Orin and I aren't together. I've seen other people, though we haven't exactly discussed that, and I'm sure he has too. I *hope* he has too. I may not have been with any men since him, but that doesn't mean I haven't been with any *people*. And if I told the internet that in my own defense, it would backfire hilariously. Horrendously. Both.

It was never just a story. We were people from the start. And now we're people getting taken out of context and reduced to our actions, without their intentions. Because what do intentions matter, when facts are facts?

Fact: Orin can't stay in his apartment without fear of being victim to a crime, and the police have put him up in a hotel.

Fact: Alain and Jackie are out, and I can't tell Laura about this without looking like the manipulative jerk I clearly am.

Fact: Orin has already been informed by his professors that he needs to attend a hearing on Monday to see whether they'll allow him to continue to teach.

Fact: It's all my fault.

Fact: I need to not be me right now, or else I'll go insane.

CHAPTER TWELVE

I t's Daphnis's first time at Red Stamp, but it isn't mine: I come to watch Alain about once a month. It's his home bar, and it's one of those places where it's relatively tame Drag Bingo until midnight and the real show doesn't start until one. On weeknights. In the part of the West Village where the people who can afford to live here are too old to be the target audience.

By the time I get off the subway, running local, it's twelve thirty. I probably still have a chance of catching Alain backstage, or at least I can track down Jackie. And even if I can't, I don't want to be alone right now, and alone is impossible at a drag bar.

The bouncer cards me, but he's not the kind of person that blinks twice when the ID doesn't match the presentation. In this hoodie, the worst I look like I'm doing is selling drugs, not heckling the queens, which is what they're really concerned about. So in I go, to find the warm-up act working the room to "Hollaback Girl" and the drunk bachelorettes in the audience shrieking along. And the only reason I can see up to the stage is that the queen is on it, since everyone else on the ground is packed in like sardines. Oh yeah, it's Friday. The rest of the world has only two nights off, and this is one of them. So I have a choice: I can try to unearth Jackie from this morass, which is like finding the bean in a King Cake, or I can go for the stage door and try to grab Alain before he goes on.

Stage door it is.

I start fighting through the crowd. You'd think it would be easier to cut carve myself some space *away* from the bar, but nope. The stage door is against the wall beside the stage, of course, and it's even odds that I get stepped on by treads or stilettos on the way. "Hollaback Girl" finishes—I make sure to applaud, even though I didn't really watch, because fuck do I know what it feels like to play to dead space—and the emcee, Alain's frenemy Lyta Touché Mizrahi (aka Steve), starts introducing the next act.

"Remember, youse," Lyta snickers into the microphone, "the girl that gets the most love during amateur hour gets a main-stage gig next week! That's right, we mopped the Applause-O-Meter straight from *Hairspray*'s storage unit. And speaking of *Hairspray*, our next warm-up is a whole lot of woman: give it up for Babs Bulgolgi!"

I'm still a good twenty feet from the stage door, and Babs apparently comes equipped with a cheering section (desination: my ear), but I don't mind. Babs is totally my type: Alain's height at least but squishy all over, with a flawless face and well-stuffed booty shorts. "*Ahnasaeyo!*" she trills into the microphone. "I'm the bubbly Babs Bulgogi. Do you like bulgogi too?"

Of course the response to *Do you like marinated prime rib?* in a gay bar is deafening.

"Oh good," she says, pushing her big breasts together and swiveling side to side like a middle school girl in one of Jackie's anime. "Some might like it dry rub! But me, I like it—"

A bucket of water upends from the ceiling, right on her head.

It must have been planned, because all I can make out of the lip sync is about her liking it *wet* specifically, but some of the shrieking in the front row isn't of the cheering variety and I'm having an even harder time fighting my way to the stage door. The crowd pushes back. And just as I think I'm making some progress, one of the now-somewhat-damp bachelorettes collides with me chest-first. And slips.

I catch her. "Sorry!"

She must hear me over the crowd, because she shouts back, "Thanks! But! She splashed my drink!"

Oh. Sure enough, it's not just water on this girl's ivory silk shirt: the spreading stain is deep cosmopolitan pink. I'm not going to make it to the stage door anyway, so I might as well help her out. It's what I'd want someone to do for me. "C'mon," I tell her, loud as I can, then take her by the wrist and start shouldering a path back out the way

I came. She's short—not as short as Jackie, but definitely shorter than I am—so I probably just doubled her stain-removal chances by being in the right place since all these queens in heels can see more than the top of my head as I clear a path.

Babs's lip sync is still going on by the time I tug the bachelorette into the bathroom corridor. You'd think a drag club wouldn't have gendered bathrooms, but this one does. Then again, *bathroom with gloryholes* and *bathroom without gloryholes* doesn't quite have the same ring to it. I bring her to the women's bathroom, which actually doesn't have a line in front of it, and let go of her wrist. "Sorry if I was rough."

"Not at all!" She smiles, but shoulders right past me into the bathroom. "I wouldn't have made it very far. You're quite chivalrous. Let me buy you a drink, okay?"

I barely get the time to say, "There's no need," before the bathroom door shuts.

She takes her time, and I don't get asked if I'm waiting by the next girl to go in. Babs's set ends, and she gets a decent amount of applause, and Lyta announces the next amateur. Maybe if I wait here long enough Jackie'll need to use the place and I can find her instead of Alain. She's got a bladder the size of a peanut.

During the last chorus of "Love on Top," the bachelorette emerges from the bathroom, her shirt now uniformly wet and translucent but no longer stained pink. Now that she isn't in a rush I can get a look at her face, and she's cute and femme, my age or a little younger, with wispy black hair and a pencil skirt and a tastefully visible lace bralette.

"Thanks again," she says. "Didn't mean to keep you waiting."

It's not a good idea to say that I wasn't waiting for her—and, well, I partway was—so I shake my head and smile back. "It's no trouble. I'm mostly here to see my roommate, and he's not on yet."

"It's cool that you're being so supportive." She holds out a hand. "Morgan."

"Daphnis." Is my handshake manly enough? I don't want to be forceful, just confident. Either way, I try to let go courteously. "*Enchanté*."

She brightens up immediately and asks, in French, "Are you for real?"

I clearly made the right decision coming out here tonight.

Over our first round of drinks—and yes, she was drinking vodka and cranberry—Morgan reveals that she's down from Quebec for her cousin's Brooklyn wedding. "But they all speak so fast," she says, "and it hasn't quite been my scene so far. This city. Not that I can find my way around it."

"It's a lot," I agree. "When I first moved to the US, my parents worked at the United Nations, but we drove everywhere. I didn't take the subway at all until I moved here after college."

"Do they still work at the UN?"

"No, they're back in France now. They're angling for an assignment to Australia next. Good thing they waited—my accent would be *really* messed up if I'd gone with them."

Over the second round of drinks—I switch beers, the local's too sweet—Morgan gets to talking about her family and the wedding drama. She's got a lot to say about bridesmaid dresses and how thankful she is that the trend right now is to let the lineup pick their own, but her cousin went with that new trend, "Everyone gets the same wrap dress, just ties it differently. But the other bridesmaids are flat as pancakes, and I have to wear one of those gross bandeaus under mine. Like the girl in Star Wars but less cool."

I commiserate. "I've never had to worry about that myself, but that sounds awful. Then again, Daisy Ridley did look hot in it, so it can't be that bad."

"You have a point," she says. "I'll try and work something out. Maybe Katie can have a go tying it for me, if she's not too stressed out tomorrow."

Over the third round of drinks, she finishes the litany of wedding shenanigans and starts telling me about the bachelorette party, which has wound up here after a long day at a spa, then a horrendously expensive seafood dinner, "And thank god the rehearsal dinner isn't until seven tomorrow because I think Olivia is gonna keep us here until four."

"She probably is. Alain usually doesn't get back until six."

She leans in, as much awkward as conspiratorial. "So is he your roommate or your . . ."

Ha, I've had to answer this about Alain and me before. "No, just roommate. We're firmly not interested in each other." Alain *has* been with girls, I think twice—in college—but he's pretty sure he never will be again. And I, well.

"Oh," Morgan says. "Good."

We miss Alain's first set completely. He's going to kill me. And then congratulate me because after round four Morgan asks me to accompany her outside for a cigarette, then proceeds to not light up, but instead grabs me by the ties of my hoodie and shoves me into the alleyway wall, then comes up on her toes to kiss me stupid.

Fuck yes. I'm not turning that down. And she's just the right kind of bossy, so I let her know I like it. It's been far too long since I've kissed anyone, longer since I've kissed anyone who spoke French, and that's a childish pun right there but I give no shits. Her shirt is still damp and it ruches up on mine, comes untucked. She says that's permission. I slide my hands up under it, and the high, breathless sounds she pants into my neck are peppered with words, *yes* in both the languages I know.

It's going to be fine. I'm going to be fine.

Her hip grinds into my groin. "How much of an exhibitionist are you?"

I smirk and pinch her. "I'm an actor."

"Great. You go up," she whispers, "I'll go down," and she unbuttons my jeans.

Maybe I've had one too many beers to put two and two together. But when she finds nothing, she makes a great deal of ado.

And reels back all the way to the opposite alley wall. "You're a *lesbian*?"

My mouth drops open, but no words come out. On the one hand, I should be ecstatic that I pass. On the other, *who the fuck goes to a drag show looking to hook up with a straight cis guy?*

The same type of person who likes to bludgeon people with her purse, apparently.

Ow.

CHAPTER THIRTEEN

I was wrong: Alain neither kills me nor congratulates me. He just walks me home. Doesn't bother taking off his makeup, just throws on his street clothes and ties back his wig and lets me lean against his shoulder on the subway. Jackie wasn't even at Red Stamp, he says; she ran into a fangirl in the Village and split off to hit up the Cubbyhole instead. I should have texted. I shouldn't have tried to surprise them. He says that, and I hear decisively *I should have been man enough to pick up my phone instead of hiding from Orin and the collective bullshit of the internet.*

But I'm not a man.

It's not that Alain is saying these things: *should* and *shouldn't* and *man up*. Those are contextually clear. It's just that Alain denying that this is one hundred percent my fault is because he's my friend and that's what friends do, so it's bullshit. Friends issue platitudes to make us feel better. Friends say we're wonderful no matter what we are. Friends warn you when they're keeping it real and break the bad news to you delicately, at a convenient time, and since no time is convenient, Alain and Jackie and Orin can't just tell me I'm a fuckup wearing someone else's pants. At the end of the day I am a fragile human being and my sanity can't take them lending voice to criticism, however obvious.

I appreciate what they can do, what they *are* doing. Alain texts Jackie and tells her he's got this and everyone's safe. Alain walks me off the subway with his arm around my shoulders so I don't fall over. Alain lets me mope around the apartment like an idiot while he gets out of drag and lets me tell him what I can of the whole story (a rotten contradiction in terms, but hey, so's *safe space*). I explain that Orin got doxxed and is spending the night with Rochester's Finest and definitely not in a tawdry gay porno way, and that I don't even know everything that's happened but the horde hasn't targeted me yet, and I just wanted to get out of the house and unplug and not worry about the fucking internet.

Alain tough loves at me for half an hour. Okay. I *should* be worried. I *should* be with people, yes, and probably *should* Cut the Cord and go internet cold turkey, but I can't pretend I'm not the droids they're looking for. I am what I am. Even if I'm being Daphnis, I'm still Fatiguee. And Daphne. And they *are* going to find me, and I *am* going to be exactly what they say I am, because that is how the world works.

I don't cry. I shake, and there's a good ten minutes where I can't actually *say* anything, but I don't cry. And when Alain asks if I want him to call out of work tomorrow, I'm perfectly capable of telling him he doesn't have to. I'll be fine. He shouldn't lose money over my drama. Enough people already have.

The latest inventory on Fatiguee's hate mail is two hundred thirty-one thousand eight hundred fifty-six. I know this because I've started reading them all.

I have to wonder how much the server can take, but then, we live in an age of cloud storage. My alotted space in this world is just one infinitesimal pocket of air in the dataspere. I am only as significant as other people make me. My corner of the sky might be radioactive enough to give someone cancer. Then again, what doesn't give someone cancer?

At least it's seven in the morning now, the dead hour. Even the West Coast must sleep, and the Europeans haven't logged on yet, and the Pan-Pacific aren't that well represented in Altestis, so if they're here, they're not bothering me.

Regnabo, regno, regnavi, sum sine regno. The unrest in what was my realm must break, if just to preserve the tension. Fatiguee's exile to Sachem's keep is so easy to picture, so straightforward to direct. She paces the halls alone, half asleep like Lady Macbeth, seeing ghosts and daggers around every corner. It is, perhaps, what she deserves. I could write that down if I had the brainspace; it's not a bad image. But every other word up here is on my screen, and no one wants to hear from the woman they're all describing. I wouldn't want to hear from her either.

After the first hundred, I start forgetting to screencap them. After the next hundred, I don't bother trying. Accept. Read. Block. Delete. Accept. Read. Block. Delete. Acceptance isn't only implicit, it's written into the code. I accept that all these things are true. Fatiguee is a whore. Fatiguee should fuck off and fuck Sachem. Fatiguee is living on borrowed time.

Delete one email, two more spring forth. This is pointless. This is a holding pattern that doesn't care whether I run out of gas two thousand feet in the air. An exercise in absurdism. If I don't log on and play, that asshole from Publicity gets to gloat and I lose the game I tried to make. If I log on, I don't get to play, just delete a hundred thousand missives which instantly replenish like an undead horde. And if I opt out, they'll come for me anyway, and I'll have done nothing to defend myself, and I am what they say.

I am what they say.

Jackie didn't get Alain's text until this morning, so apparently she had a much better night than I did. She comes in to check on me at eleven or so. Alain told her most of it, she says, so if I don't want to talk about it, that's okay. She brought doughnuts from one of those pretentious shops in the wilds of Brooklyn, so clearly she didn't stay at the Cubbyhole for long. I tell her I'm glad I didn't ruin her night.

Since I don't want to read these shame spiral emails in front of her—if I didn't ruin her night, why ruin her morning?—I let her lead me into the kitchen where she makes coffee and ascertains that yes, I will consume a doughnut. Perhaps more than one doughnut. Alain wakes up at the smell of coffee and joins us for just long enough to fill in the rest of the gaps in Jackie's knowledge.

Then Jackie checks Twitter.

#EthicalReign is trending.

Five doughnuts and the subsequent sugar crash later, I fall asleep on the couch. Then wake up, knock on Jackie's door to inform her I'm alive, and crash on the bed for another two hours or so. It's ten at night, so there's really no point in pretending I'm going to leave the house today, so I watch clips from *Company* on my phone until the battery dies.

Did Neil Patrick Harris ever deal with this shit?

Alain comes home and trips over the coatrack. I was already awake, sort of. Mostly. Wakefulness is relative. It's six in the morning and we're out of doughnuts.

I straighten up all the fallen coats, then just don't stop cleaning until Jackie wakes up. Or until after Jackie wakes up, technically, since she calls me into the kitchen to sous-chef for her. I chop onions and still don't cry. An elaborate brunch sounds like an excellent idea in theory, but in practice it's a whole lot of disparate fractal moments that don't really line up. The bacon is Canadian. So was Morgan, whose name I will probably never forget even though she's just a hookup that went south. Or, more precisely, didn't. It's not her fault. It's mine, like everything else. And I assumed she was okay with it. With me. Of whom assuming made an ass.

This elaborate brunch is getting out of control. Jackie's making hollandaise sauce. I hope she's the one to poach the eggs; I suck.

That's also a general statement. With several hundred thousand corroborations on the internet.

I wonder how my parents are doing.
Australia sounds like a brilliant idea.

My breath still smells like eggs Benedict, and I only now get the joke.

It's Alain's turn to pick the entertainment. And entertainment is, like wakefulness, a relative term. We end up watching the legendarily crap CGI movie tie-in to one of his favorite video games and taking a swig every time someone's hair doesn't move how it's supposed to. Somehow, no one gets alcohol poisoning. Even more miraculously, no one falls asleep.

But then Jackie gets an idea for her next fanfic, and Alain remembers a thing he has to fix about that monstrous green wig, so I head back to my room and log on.

Fatiguee. Not Bannedict. To check the numbers, that's all.

Three hundred thousand and what the fuck ever. The trickle seems to be slowing down. Maybe I've blocked enough of them that they've run out of fake IP addresses. Either way, it's less awful than I thought it would be. In terms of quantity, at least. Not in terms of content.

I feel like that passage in *The Princess Bride* about the hats. They cut it out of the movie, but there was this amazing ten-page litany of all the headgear this one courtier wore, I think the author suspected that any reader would just skim and skip and get to the good parts, but then there was a punchline. She's bald. Ten pages of individual hat descriptions don't matter, but ten *pages* of *hats* do, regardless of content or quality. If I translate it like a playwright, it's like saying *[Business.]* It worked for the Marx brothers. Let them improvise until Harpo does something funny. *[Business with a hat.]* *[Business with a plunger.]* *[Business with a shelf of cream pies and a cockatiel.]* *[Business with a troll.]*

Maybe I can make this funny. Hell, that's what I did with the *Annals*. Considering that a couple got divorced IRL over my court game, some events needed to be recontextualized for comic effect. I *have* a sense of humor in here somewhere. I could laugh at the sheer amount of people who want me raped or dead or both, and I could laugh at this pretense of a gender crisis that's just turning me into even more of a lying twat, and I could laugh at the fact that I'm going insane over a literal shared illusion run by a corrupt organization in the role of a distant and incomprehensible unfeeling god.

Nope.

[Business with a vibrator.]

Does it log me for play hours when I leave the game running overnight? I guess I'll find out when *Monsieur Publicité* decides to revoke my award. Either way, I wake to the sound of spamming messages. Not email missives, chat requests, with that little *ding* and conveniently sized window.

It takes me four of those pings to get out of bed and another two to make it to the computer.

It's Orin.

[Text] [Voice] [Video]

Voice. I might still be drunk from yesterday. I can't imagine I look sober either. God, why do I even care?

"Hey."

"Hey yourself." He's more garbled through the computer than he would be through my phone. Where the fuck *is* my phone? "You're not answering my calls," he says.

". . . Shit, I forgot to recharge since . . . I think Saturday."

"You *think* Saturday?"

"What day is it?"

"Monday, Daphne. I just got out of the hearing."

I could say, *Then yes, Saturday*, but the hearing is much more important. "Is it going to be—"

"I've negotiated an unpaid leave of absence," he says, before I even finish. "They might let me back in the spring. Or next fall. However long it takes for this to blow over, they said. The IRB has to go over my file."

"They *believed* that bullshit?"

"It's not, Daphne. It's not all bullshit."

I swear, my heart has the circulatory equivalent of a wi-fi hiccough.

Orin takes the kind of deep breath that I wish I could. "Philosophy departments don't usually require surveys, since we mostly deal in past sources and anecdata. But if I'm studying gameplay and live practice, anecdata doesn't cut it. If I can't draw up consent forms for every player I've ever worked with, I can't legally use that as data in my dissertation. So the trolls have a point. Not about you, but about me."

"But they never would have come after you if it weren't for me. Orin, I'm so sorry—"

"It's not your fault. I promise it's not your fault."

"No, it's—"

"I walked into this." He only raises his voice a little. Why does it scare me so much? "Please, don't blame yourself. If I hadn't written those posts in the first place, they wouldn't have come after me, that's true. But I didn't just do this for you. And the IRB problem has nothing to do with you. I'm a grown man. I don't intend to blame you at all."

"That makes one of us," I could have chosen not to say. Too late.

"At least there's a bright side," he says. I'm not sure if he's ignoring what I said or if he didn't hear me. "If I don't have to teach, and I have to get a new place to live anyway, I can get out of Rochester. Come back to civilization. Maybe back to Long Island with my parents, but . . ."

No, that's not a wi-fi hiccough in my heart. It's a dead zone. I know *exactly* where this is going, and I can't stop him saying it.

". . . I could come be with you in NYC."

Yep. He said it. He said it, and now he can't take it back. And I can't say anything.

"I could protect you," he goes on, like he doesn't even *know* how much I *don't want to hear this*. "And we could get through this together. Like we're supposed to deal with this together. No more distance. No more games."

A sheer wall of *no* comes crashing down around me. It takes Orin responding for me to realize I said it aloud. No. *No.* "No."

I can't take that back either.

"I know you're worried about them finding you too, but with the two of us together we could—"

"No, Orin. I mean. No. I don't want you to come here."

"Well, you're right, they could still track us if we were together, but—"

I barely have the control to keep this in English. "No. It's not about them. It's about you. I don't want *you* to come *here*."

"But Daphne—"

"I'm not what you think I am." I'm not what you say I am. Dominant perception. Casting. A headshot. A person worth fighting for. "I'm— Orin, I can't do this. I can't deal with this. And you're not helping."

"I know I'm not. But I *want* to."

"You're not helping the right person."

"I could be if she'd just *let me!*"

Yes, he did shout. First I'd never seen him panic. Now I've heard him shout, not mere obscenities at a difficult boss or unsolicited aggro. He shouted. At me.

No. At *her*. At this person he sees, who he touched once, three years ago, and has been seeing ever since, no matter how far away she is, no matter what she's become without him. At the girl in the photo on the internet. At the actress.

"Daphne," he says, and either the speakers are crap or he really is shaking, "I'm sorry. But you're so important to me. And I want—"

Combat windows explode all over the screen. Lowslip is under siege. Krozin and the Horde, of course.

Well, that's as good an exit cue as any.

I log out.

And when I charge my phone, I block Orin across platforms.

CHAPTER FOURTEEN

Seeing as I'm doing really stupid things on lots of stress and no sleep, I may as well fuck everything up completely. *I have nothing left to lose.*

I swear that wasn't the first thought in my mind when I got dressed to go out, literally as soon as I hung up on Orin. I told Jackie that I'm not logging on to *ER* anymore, and she said that sounds like a good idea. That I should go to work. Which is possibly one of those really stupid things I'm doing on a stress/sleep cocktail, but maybe in dance class I don't have to impress anyone. I don't have to fight people who'd never let me win. I *don't* tell Jackie about Orin because I still don't know what the fuck is going on with that, except that I don't want anything at all to be going on with that. And it's not me he's interested in anyway. He wants Daphne.

I never want to be Daphne again.

I've got so much more free time on my hands this week without engaging with *Eternal Reign*. I make it to all of my dance classes and two out of three stage combat seminars. A whole lot of people compliment me on the hair, and Alain teaches me how to use his electric razor so I can keep the sides shaved. The scar only gets one ingrown hair, and it hurts like hell—and so does plucking it out with a sterilized tweezer, *ow*—but that's an adventure the real world can take.

And I schedule a meeting with my agent for Wednesday morning. On the phone, not over email, like it's the nineties.

So into Julio's office I stroll, in an outfit that Alain mostly picked out: black jeans, jacket over hoodie over tank over binder, hair artfully mussed, no makeup. I look like the bad boy in an a capella group, but hey, that's current. The receptionist doesn't recognize me, so I give her my last name and wait.

I don't have a script for this, but I do have key points. I want to talk options. I want to clarify what happened last week with *An American in Paris*. And I want to stay in this profession, just change the package.

Maybe I should have packed. I don't think I have time to stuff a sports bra into my underwear. But it would get my point across.

The receptionist tells me that Julio will see me now. I get up, nod a thanks, and prepare to audition all over again.

"—Daphne?" he says, going Muppet-eyed and double-taking, the whole nine yards.

"*Bounjour,*" I say, in the same lower voice I tried with Laura.

"Well, hello *Boys Don't Cry!*" He reaches across his desk to shake my hand, then goes to the kettle in the corner. "Did you get a nonunion role, or what?"

"No. But that's part of what I want to discuss."

"Good, good. Green tea?"

"Sure."

He fusses about for a minute, then hands me a mug with the bag still in. Instead of sitting down behind his desk, he perches on the edge, looks down at me like a tactical map. "So. Talk to me."

I take a breath, and improvise a monologue from the framework I've been obsessing over for the last couple of days. At least. "First, I want to apologize for *An American in Paris*—"

"No need to apologize for roles you didn't get," he waves off. "I've told you before, that's all them, not you."

"—but it brought up some concerns that I've been. Um. Fighting with, these past few weeks." This time, he doesn't interrupt me, just waits while I take a sip of tea. Still too hot, and not quite green enough. "I definitely want to keep trying to get out there. But I'm not sure going for chorus girl roles is the way to do it."

"Daphne, everyone has to put in their time." He sighs. It's the spiel he gives all the poor corps angling for their big breaks and wondering why they haven't gotten their names in lights yet. That's not the problem here, and he needs to know it.

"No. I'm not saying that I don't want to accept small parts. But." I gesture at what I'm wearing. "Chorus *girl* might not be the right direction."

Let it not be said that my agent doesn't have eyes. He looks me over again, this time lingering on the hair, then the face, then the chest. "Go on."

"At that call, they asked me to be more feminine. Apparently I wasn't feminine enough. It's not the first time I've been wrong for an ingénue role. You have my reviews from Brenda, and that whole thing with *Carousel*. And yes, I can dance, but that's not limited to women."

"You can't sing male roles even if you can dance them, and you can't do lifts."

"Yet," I point out. "And there are men who can't do lifts either."

"True." He leans back, crosses his arms. "So do you want me to think of you as a trans actor?"

"I'm not sure," I admit. "But I think I'd feel better if you stopped thinking of me as an actress."

He nods. Oh good, that's all it took. This is the best thing to happen to me since that chat with Laura, and it's not costing me my career. I can keep trying. I can keep going.

"All right," Julio says. "I just want you to be aware that this is a risk."

"It's always a risk."

"Yes, but usually the devil you know beats the devil you don't."

"Not this time. And hey, you could cast me in *Side Show* with very little trouble."

"After how the revival flopped? Fat chance." But he's smiling, and when he rounds the desk to sit down and open my file, he doesn't stop or cringe or shudder. "So. First, you're going to need new headshots. That's at your own expense, and I want them in two weeks. I'll insist that you bleach the dye out or go natural, but you can keep the cut, it's trendy. And it's flattering."

"Fine—and thank you."

"New pronouns?"

"Haven't thought about it, actually. I'm not sure I care."

He makes a note. "I'll start keeping an eye out for androgyne-specific roles. Keep training your upper body and ask your dance instructor to teach you some lifts, and then maybe we can expand your bids to men's chorus and character roles. And you have to keep a lookout as well; I can't do everything for you. If you see something you want to gun for, tell me and I'll help us come up with a pitch. And I warn you, you may have more success in LA."

"I'll consider it."

"Good. A couple more questions. Can I pitch you for stunt work? A lot of trans actors make real money subbing in for teenagers who can't legally do their own stunts."

Wait, really? "Yes. Yes, definitely." I hadn't thought of that, and while it's a little outdated and ideologically disturbing, he's not exaggerating about it being good money, and I'm not taking all these stage combat classes for nothing.

"Great, that's an excellent way in for you. Next question: are you going to go on T?"

The only answer to that is, "I don't know."

"All right. If you start considering it, please keep me in the loop. It can mess with your weight, and your voice, especially when you start taking it as old as you are, and that changes your options. And I warn you, even taking stunt work into account, there are a lot fewer options than there would be if you wanted to keep trying for the chorus line."

I nod. There are still expectations. It's still based on What They See. But these seem like much easier boxes to check and things to keep in mind than the ones I dealt with last week.

He doesn't keep me much longer after that; he recommends some new song cuts, promises to email the other trans actors he's worked with in the past—both of whom have since moved to LA for film work—and put me in touch, and gives me a list of things to take care of before we meet again, after I get back from GeeKon. This may be the best meeting I've had with him since he signed me in the first place. Well, it *is* a new signing, from a certain point of view.

"Oh, I almost forgot," he says on my way out the door. "Will you be using a new stage name?"

It's that simple. I had no idea it was that simple.

"Daphnis," I answer, and spell it out while he writes it down.

"Good. I'll make sure it isn't taken. And break a leg, Daphnis. See you on the sixteenth."

I don't need to force this smile; it's happening all on its own. "Thank you. And especially. . . for taking me seriously."

"It's a serious business," he demurs. "Go on. Just keep me in the loop."

CHAPTER FIFTEEN

"How did it go?" Jackie asks, literally the second I walk in the door. I tell her.

Somehow, Alain is still the first one to flying tackle me. For fuck's sake. He wasn't even in the room.

Well, Alain said it called for a celebration. Which is how we wind up at Red Stamp on his night off. Jackie said she's too much in the writing groove to come out, but Alain's just glad to show up without having to do makeup for four hours and stay out until sunrise, and I'm just *glad*.

And since he's not Ivy tonight, when he starts hitting on people, it's one hundred percent genuine.

So he snags us a table on the second floor (right behind the RAIN GOE$ HERE sign on the railing), and we end up sharing it with Whitney, the shorter and darker of the two, who says, "And no, that's not my drag name. And this is Ivan."

Ivan extends a hand, and I shake it. "Daphnis."

"Another one of Alain's expats?" he asks, no derision evident.

I nod. "And you?"

"No, I'm first generation. We still speak Russian at home, though."

Ivan doesn't have much of an accent, but he definitely looks like a lot of the rich children of NATO advocates I used to meet at my parents' work parties—at least as pale as Jackie, but with nearly black hair instead of her auburn, with that really solid cut to his jaw and, for lack of a better term, resting bitchface. And he sits there while

Alain and Whitney trade drag gossip, which starts off as a game of Who's Screwing Whom and segues into an admittedly hilarious story involving Whitney, his ex-boyfriend, a metal cock ring, a trip to the emergency room in Thailand, and a hacksaw.

"I think they still put him under general anesthesia," Whitney concludes.

I laugh so hard my throat hurts. Alain manages to stop long enough to say, "Okay, the next round's on me. I'm stealing that story."

"Don't you fucking dare, Ivy," Whitney says, in that not-certain-how-sarcastic way that sets off klaxons in my head.

Alain scoffs, trying to swivel around the chairs without knocking into anyone else. "Just for that I'm pissing in yours. It's not Ivy unless I'm tucked."

Whitney puts up his hands in surrender. "Whatever turns you on, *Felicia*."

Alain grins and flips him off, but goes to buy the drinks anyway.

I'm still not sure I get it, but hey. It works for them.

"I will never understand you drag queens," Ivan says. This may be the first thing he's said since before Whitney's lurid story. It's also a slightly stronger echo of what's in my head, which is, frankly surprising.

Whitney pats him on the shoulder condescendingly. "It's just like you with your smack talk."

"No, it's not." Ivan folds his hands around his pint, rolls his eyes. "When I tell the cleric he's a pussy, I mean he's a pussy. And he needs to get his elf ass over here or the whole raid's going to shit."

Some serious key words here: *Cleric. Elf. Raid.*

I find myself asking, "What MMO?"

Ivan lights up immediately. He's got nice eyes, strangely, when they're not trying to find cracks in the hardwood. "*Kingdom of Elves*, these days. You?"

"*Eternal Reign*," I say before I can quite stop myself, but it doesn't hurt. "I'm taking a break, though."

He smiles. "I don't blame you, with all that hashtag bullshit going down."

"Oh, fuck me," Whitney groans. "Not this shit again."

I laugh, but Ivan glares at Whitney with DreamWorks eyebrows. "Hey, you're the one making me sit through a drag show, the least you can do is let me talk with the one gaymer I've found here who isn't Babs."

"Fair, fair. Fuck, you two sound like you're dropping code in a bathhouse."

"Or flagging," Ivan says.

That's actually pretty funny. "Like an eight-bit flag in the left pocket means old school top," I offer.

Ivan laughs and slaps the table. "Or a white handprint means Horde only."

"Three colors twisted means looking for group!"

"Red cross on the left: looking for paladin play!"

"And red on the right if you're down to Ret pally!"

Whitney pitches forward, still groaning, and raps his head on the table a couple of times. "You fucking nerds."

It's Ivan's turn to pat Whitney consolingly. "My turn to leave you out. Go talk about lipstick with Ivy."

"Alain," I correct. But since the conversation should probably get back on track so no one gets insulted, I point out, "I basically *am* flagging." I twist enough to show the back of my hoodie: *OPALESCE SURVIVOR, 3637 C.E.*

"No way," Ivan leans in. "You did *Periapta*?"

"For two years."

"Oh shit, you got started." Alain arrives, balancing four beers, one of which *does* look slightly yellower than the rest. (Alain's pulled that trick on us since high school. It's either sour mix or Crystal Light, whichever's handy.) He sets that one down in front of Whitney. "Here, *ma chérie*."

"You're a sick fuck." He drinks anyway. "Save me from these geeks."

"Not if you're calling me a sick fuck."

"It's fine," Ivan says, pushing back his chair. "We can leave you two alone. It's too loud in here to talk anyway." He takes two of the pints, and cocks his head at me. "Outside okay?"

"Yeah." I get up and grab my jacket and phone. "I'm up for some war stories."

"Up," he asks, pointedly, "or *down*?"

I laugh, but before I can answer he's already sidestepping the crowd on the way to the stairs. He's about Alain's height but broader, so he cuts an easier path than I managed last week, and gets us out to the sidewalk without much trouble and with no spillage. Only then does he hand me my beer.

"You don't mind," he mutters, "do you?"

I shake my head and take a sip. "You're right that it's hard to talk in there."

"They're like the cheerleaders in the school cafeteria," he agrees.

"Guess I'm lucky we didn't have any in ours."

"Is that how you know Alain?"

I get through a condensed version of the Musketqueers origin story, which leads to Ivan relating his experiences in his strict-as-hell Eastern Orthodox school, which leads straight back to how he got into gaming. And how long we've been gaming, which is about the same length of time, though we've never really crossed into each other's orbit. We finish our beers, but neither of us makes a move to go back in for more, so he sets his pint under the bouncer's folding chair and I follow suit, and we just keep going.

"I think it just hit me at the best time," Ivan says. "You know, finding a place I could cut loose. You're lucky you had Alain and that girl, even if he's a console twink."

He smiles, so I smile back. "Having people let you be you makes a huge difference."

"Exactly. I remember my first LAN party. And my first con. Those guys just got that I was here to have a good time and kill some aliens. But on top of that, you know." He gestures at the entrance to the bar. "Gamer and Grindr don't usually overlap. And when they do it's all that buzzword activist shit."

I am immediately, palpably glad that I have had only two drinks.

List in my head time. Item one: *Buzzword activist shit*. He didn't say *social justice warrior*. I'm not sure if that makes it easier or harder to tell whether he's pissed off or only jaded. Item two: he's already proven himself awkward and is just trying to find someone to commiserate with, so I can maybe give him the benefit of the doubt. Item three: we're at a gay bar for fuck's sake, it should be a safe place for him to say what he thinks. But item four: we're standing *outside* the bar because he called Alain and Whitney loud queens. Five: those kind of insults are how the aforementioned loud queens talk to each other. Six: I can very easily translate what he's saying as *Gamer means more to me than gay but gay is important too.* If it's only that I completely understand.

"It's not all buzzwords, but I know what you're getting at," I settle on. Benefit of the doubt, for now. It's all right to disagree. "But I guess that if you're going somewhere where gay is assumed, you have to look for a gamer. And the other way around."

"Yeah, but when both get assumed?" He scoffs through his teeth. "They're all lesbians. Or so—"

Shrieks and applause ring out from the bar, into the street. The show must be starting.

Ivan groans. "Looks like all women are loud, even fake ones."

Item seven: he doesn't think I'm a woman. Which is, in a strictly gender-confirming sense, awesome.

Item eight: ABORT ABORT ABORT.

I start edging toward the bouncer, but Ivan doesn't seem to pick up on it. "It's just like on the internet. Wait—you play *Eternal Reign*, right? Did you hear about that crazy bitch and the journalist?"

Abort is not an option. All systems failing. My body has informed me: *I'm afraid I can't do that, Daphnis.*

Ivan must think I've said something, or he must be interpreting my expression for a different kind of *oh shit*, because he keeps talking. "Oh yeah, you're taking a break. This girl won a company contest or something, then quit and let her boyfriend hold on to the guild, and when someone stormed their base this guy made a huge stink about it. It's the *same fucking thing*, every time. And it's always a fucking girl, trying to make the game about something not gaming." He grimaces and hisses through his teeth. "I'd find that cunt and give her what for myself if I could. Almost joined *Eternal Reign* to do it—an old friend of mine's ankle-deep and tried to recruit me to the cause, but I've got a con to save up for. Besides, I'd rather just watch the trainwreck. Krozin's already got his hands full trying to keep shit under control."

Krozin.

Krozin.

"Wait, you know Krozin?" he asks.

Shit, I said that aloud. "Um. Yeah. Periapta."

"Right, he was big back then too."

Okay. I'm safe. I should invent an excuse and go. I should have invented an excuse and gone *thirty-five minutes ago*. My flight response isn't working. Friend Computer is singing, merrily, *You'll never walk alone!* A sperm whale is falling from the sky. The petunias are chagrined.

"I wish games were still like that. None of this romance-novel tie-in crap. This cunt wants to write let's-all-fuck-Shepard for Bioware so fucking much she's inflicting it on people who want to play a real MMO. It used to be about *games*."

What I mean to say is, *It stopped being a game when it ruined my life.*

What I actually say is, "It's not a romance novel, it's bluebooking, and even if it were it's my fucking business, not yours."

The effect of those words on Ivan is immediate. A cab wheels by behind him, and the high beams leave shadows behind. All the openness, all the camaraderie in his expression is gone. He's just as uncomfortable and bewildered as he was upstairs.

Then he squints at me.

"You're her," he says, barely audible in the chatter of the line. "You're Fatiguee."

Fight-or-flight kicks in, *way* behind schedule, and I definitely run in the wrong direction because he steps in to block me. Our shoulders clash, and he reels back, almost to the line at the door. The bouncer notices. If I've noticed the bouncer noticing, I'm watching too much and running too little.

Or maybe I noticed just in time: Ivan is lifting his phone to take a picture.

I turn tail. I don't even know which way I'm going, but all roads lead to a subway. He's following me. Someone's yelling, "Get her!" and this is the kind of city where people listen. Feet pound behind me, the sidewalk crowds won't part fast enough, the Village is full even on a Wednesday night, and this is all my fault. I make it to the avenue, against the light, crowd on the left, traffic on the right—

He grabs me by the hood and yanks me into a wall.

I haven't taken all of those stage combat classes for nothing. I know how to take a hit. I know how to fall as safely as possible. I know how to make something look like it hurts a lot more than it actually does. But this is real. It's *been* real. And this isn't a choreographed fight in a show, or a pixilated one with menus and spells. This is callback real, Twitter real, someone-might-call-the-cops real.

And as long as it's real, I am going to *really* fight back.

I wind up and sock Ivan in the face.

He staggers toward the street, but not into it. I can get away, but he might already be recording this. He's one of Krozin's trolls, or as good as, and—nope, not enough time to process that. He curses in Russian and swings for my head, fist curled around his phone. I duck, scrape my palm on the sidewalk. Someone *else* might be taping this—someone else is definitely shouting about it—but they won't know who to look for and Ivan *will*.

The next time he tries to punch me, I grab his wrist and hold on tight. He still nicks my nose, and it hurts like murder, but I refuse to let go. I twist, stomp on his instep. No, that's a miss. And he sees the next one coming, tries to use his weight to bear me down to the ground. I can work with that—I have to, he's heavier than he looks—so I try to fall as safely as I can. I think I ripped my sweatshirt. And that is definitely blood on the concrete. No matter: I slam his hand with the phone into the pavement.

He didn't see that coming, so it only takes one hit.

His phone slides toward the gutter. I crawl forward as fast as I can, and he catches my ankle but I can barely make it. There's a sewer grating in the gutter, and I hurl the phone the rest of the way. At this distance, I don't miss. The phone disappears into the black and the internet will never know.

He twists me faceup and gives me a black eye that matches his, but I'm safe.

It's a very strange time to think I'm safe.

Someone pries him off me before another punch can land, and he screams that I'll pay. I don't stick around to listen. The subway is on the other side of the street, and the light's in my favor, and I don't ever want to see Ivan again, not even in a forensic sketch. I bolt for the stairs and ignore anyone who tries to stop me, jump the turnstile, and skid into the first train that comes, no matter the direction. I'll figure out the way home once I can breathe.

As soon as I have reception, underground at twenty-third, I text Jackie and Alain.

I'm safe
Going home
Alain, watch out for Ivan
Jackie, please be awake
All for one

They both text back by the time the train hits Thirty-fourth:

One for all.

CHAPTER SIXTEEN

Jackie opens the door from the other side, while my key's still in it on mine. Nope, she's not wearing clothes, but it's almost midnight, and none of the neighbors care. She hugs me in the doorway, and I hug back until my hands stop shaking.

Then she takes the key out of the door so I don't lose it, and demands, "First three needs that come to mind."

I can let her take care of me. I basically already said I would in those texts. "A beer."

"There's a six-pack in the fridge. And?"

"Another hug?"

"Of course. And the last?"

". . . The trashiest fucking anime you have."

She laughs and hugs me again, pulls me in enough that the door shuts behind me. I make it to the couch and get out of my shoes, and she goes to the kitchen and comes back with not only the six-pack but a mug of hot water, an ice pack, and a dishtowel. Then she ducks into the bathroom and produces the first aid kit, and swipes her favorite blanket off the armchair and throws it over me. I remember the first time she did this, back in high school: I got caught up in someone else's fight (I'm pretty sure rich-kid drugs were involved), and I didn't want the cops to catch me because then my parents would have effectively jailed me even if they hadn't. Some things never change.

I crack a beer while Jackie tracks down *Weiss Kreuz* on Hulu.

It takes exactly one frame for the terribleness to ensue. After that, we just sit there for a while, watching the flower-shop-boys-slash-assassins have sexual tension with each other.

Jackie doesn't take out her laptop or mess with her phone. At the first commercial break, she opens the first aid kit and hands me an antiseptic wipe. I clean up my face and knuckles, and she dips the towel in the hot water to hand me afterward, then wraps up the ice pack for last.

"Is any of it still bleeding?"

She shakes her head. "There's a scrape on your nose. I don't think your eye was ever bleeding."

She hasn't asked me what happened. She may not at all. God, I'm so glad it's her home tonight and not Alain. Considering the riot act he read me last time, at any rate.

We make it to the end of the episode with me holding the ice pack to my face while trying to get it to work on my knuckles too, kill two birds with one stone. She lets the autoplay kick in. This show really is awful. It's exactly what I need right now.

It takes two more beers, around the commercial break of the third episode, for me to start talking.

"I can't be happy," I say.

She leans her head on my shoulder and listens.

"I mean. I feel like the universe doesn't want me to be happy. It wants to give me something good just to immediately take it away. So I can't be happy if I know that something three times worse is coming. I win the contest, I lose the game. I meet a hot girl, I can't tell her who I am. I figure something out about myself, and the whole world fights it. So nothing good comes alone."

"Not nothing," she corrects. "We're still here."

The roses of her sleeve tattoo are only beginning to come into color, but the Musketqueer one we share was completed long ago. Hers is on her chest, and all three swords peek over the edge of the blanket.

I let my head flop on top of hers. "Right. Sorry."

"You don't have to apologize. I just want you to know we're here. Even if it doesn't feel like it. You have good people that stay. So you can have good things that stay too."

"Orin's gone," I admit. "I drove him off. He wanted to come here, and I turned him down, and he started—he started making it clear he wanted more. And it's my fault for leading him on."

"No, it's not. You were friends first. Either of you could have brought it up sooner if you wanted to change that. It's not on you." She smiles, wry and small. "You just speak different languages, that's all."

"I shouldn't have gotten him into this mess."

She shakes her head. "You're not the one who attacked him. I've read every one of his posts, and I'm tracking the hashtag. Do you want to know what's going on, or are you still not comfortable?"

"No. I don't want to deal with that yet. But is he safe?"

"Yes. He's updating. So is Laura."

Relief floods my system, as cold as the pack on my eye. "Good."

The episode ends, and another string of ads begins. Jackie clicks it to mute, for now, but otherwise lets things run. "Even if you don't want to talk to Orin, you could confide in her," she suggests, like it's simple, like it's right.

"I wish I could." I don't think I meant to sigh that hard, but hey. It's not exactly in my control.

Jackie raises her eyebrows.

"I've been lying to her. Not about who I am, just . . . about who I'm not. She doesn't know I'm Fatiguee. She doesn't know I started all of this. I've kept it from her for, what, a month? A month and a half?"

"You didn't start it," Jackie says, still not-precisely-glaring, but not wavering either. "It's not about the start. It's about whether you keep going or not. And you've kept going."

"With what? With the lie?"

"It's not a lie. It's a character you play in a game." A second later, she says, like it's only just occurred to her, "It's a story."

I have to concede that point.

By the time the ice pack loses its chill, I'm about ready to drift off. Jackie seems to get it too, and pets my hair until I slump over.

The combined efforts of Alain coming home and Jackie making breakfast wake me up, however many hours later.

It smells *phenomenal*.

"Perfect timing," Alain cheers, twirling through the front door. "I can scarf those down, then finish packing."

I must not be awake, because the first thought that occurs to me is *Alain, you don't have to pack, you have a dick.*

Jackie scrapes something on a skillet. I can't see into the kitchen from here, but can hear just fine. "If you forget anything, text me. I've got room in my suitcase."

"Excellent. But I've got most of it covered. Is Daphnis packed, do you know?"

I sit up on the couch. "You could ask them. And no, I'm not."

Alain perches on the table's edge, balancing a plate with what looks like a section of frittata and a heap of fruit. "Morning, main character! *Rise and shiner,*" he adds, in English. Fucking hell, it's too early to be bilingual. "I heard you caused a timely breakup last night. Not that Whitney and that tool didn't deserve each other, but, hey. I'm sure he can find someone worse." He grins. "I'm buying all your drinks on the plane."

"The plane," I repeat.

"The plane!" he trills, in English. Like on *Fantasy Island.* "To Seattle. In six hours. If you're still doing GeeKon."

I fall off the couch.

CHAPTER SEVENTEEN

It's midnight EST, but only nine at night here in Seattle, and *shit* do I feel the difference. I napped on the second plane, and I continued that nap in the hotel room while Alain was getting into drag and Jackie still hadn't arrived yet, but I get the feeling jetlag is going to be my disadvantage for this entire weekend.

But I'm at a con. For the first time in years. And it's *fucking awesome*.

It turns out GeeKon isn't as big as NYGC: projected attendance is about twelve thousand, not twenty. The line for general badge pickup wraps around the entire exhibition hall, and there are already hundreds of people parading in costumes. I once explained to a family member—some second cousin, some party back in France—that conventions are like nerd amusement parks without the rides, and where anyone is allowed to dress like Mickey Mouse. (And lo and behold, there's King Mickey from Kingdom Hearts chatting up Godzilla on the escalator.)

Alain's going to chance the pre-reg line tomorrow afternoon, since he's got photoshoots tonight and tomorrow morning, so he comes with me and Jackie to panelist registration instead. Jackie's got a full track, two panels Friday, one Saturday, one Sunday, so they comped her badge. And I'm, well. As far as I know I can still get in for free since they haven't revoked my win.

I bring that up, and Alain—Ivy, rather, Ivy dressed as some kind of armored bunny girl archer—pats me on the arm, careful of the long, claw fingernails. "I'll get yours if they don't," she says. "You just have to promise to bring someone who tips to the drag show."

"Done." But I try not to think about it.

We get stopped every few feet for someone to take pictures of Ivy—I have to admit, she looks hot; I'd take a photo even if I didn't know which game she's from, which I don't—but make it to the panelist pickup eventually. Jackie gets signed in okay, but I'm told that yes, my name is on the list, but my file itself is at the SummerStorm booth in the exhibit hall. A con ops security officer has to escort me, but that's no problem.

"Will you be all right?" Jackie asks.

I nod. "I can text if I'm not."

"Good. I'll keep you updated of where I am. Still at the hotel, I think."

"And I'll meet you back there after my shoot," Ivy says. "It should be about an hour, maybe two if no one kicks us off the roof. I do *not* want to waste this wind."

They split off, and security takes me through the service entrance to the exhibit hall.

I've never been in a dealers' room while it's being set up, and I have to admit, some of the magic is lost. There are pockets of full assembly, but it's uncannily like being onstage with a half-painted set. The loading dock doors are open, trolleys running on the concrete between the maze of metal tables and PVC displays, some with banners, some without. The industry booths have personal carpets in cranberry red and dark blue, which you never notice when people are standing on them, waiting for autographs. A gigantic display of wigs is half-erected in the far corner, dozens of Styrofoam heads on vises clipped to chickenwire with enormous tiers of candy-colored hair. A crew of people with motorized cat-ear headphones is unloading box after box of the things onto IKEA shelving. And all the biggest industry sites are spread across the center square, a professional island in this ocean of wannabes. There's EA, and there's Square Enix USA, right next to Riot Games, and— There it is.

SummerStorm Entertainment Inc.

Security walks me over, and leans over the side table, stacked with swag and promotional banners. "Hey, Mal! I got one of your comps."

"One second," a sallow guy in a trilby answers, halfway up a ladder. He comes down, pulling a tablet from seemingly *nowhere*, and crosses over to me.

Item One: he and I are exactly the same height, probably the same weight. Weird.

Item Two: he's Malcolm Harding. *Monsieur Publicité.* The guy whose intern called me a coward.

"Name?" he asks.

"Benoit," I answer. "I'm the Novelization Contest winner."

He looks up from the tablet, which brings out more jaundice in his skin, and meets my eyes for the first time. There's a flicker of recognition, or something, and if this were theater it would be in the stage directions, but then he just turns back to the tablet and starts swiping around.

"ID," he says, extending his hand.

I take out my wallet and hand over my driver's license.

He looks between it and my face, like a bouncer on a cop-strike night. "I'm surprised you showed up," he says. Then he turns over his shoulder and says, "Chris, get her folder."

I'll ignore the *her*, since he may well mean Fatiguee, not me. The gofer ducks under one of the tables to a mini filing cabinet, comes up with a manila folder, and hands it to Harding, who then passes it to me with no ado whatsoever.

"It should all be in there," he enumerates, tapping his fingers on the tablet's edge. "Comped badge, industry panel VIP pass, six-month subscription voucher. Congratulations."

I peek in, just to be sure, and yes, all the items are there. "When is my meeting with Mr. Summers?"

He rolls his eyes. "He's not even here yet. The official panel is Sunday, right before the closing ceremonies. I'll pencil you in for after that, if you're still around."

"I don't fly out until Monday," I explain. "I'll be here."

He makes the according note on his tablet calendar, and I on mine. "Then 3 p.m. Sunday. If that changes, I'll let you know. A lot depends on Mr. Summers," he says, somewhat ominously. "He's avoiding the controversy, you know."

"I figured."

"Well," Harding says with a tip of his hat, "enjoy the con. And good luck."

I know an exit cue when I hear one, so I clip on my badge and go.

Drinking alone at a hotel bar is pretty fucking sad, but hey, I'm French. And it's still less sad than ordering one to the room, not to mention less expensive. Plus, I may be drinking alone, but I'm not drinking *alone*. At least three anime characters, two photographers, a superhero and her wife, a movie star, the Professor, and Mary Ann are here. It's more people-watching than self-medication.

That sounded like a threat from Harding. Everything from that tepid *congratulations* onward. But I could be missing things in translation, and the official statement from SummerStorm is that an intern hijacked Harding's account to dismiss me.

The way he's glued to that tablet, I doubt it. But hey. I'm here to celebrate, not sleuth. And I can't just sit in an expensive hotel room forever. I could be lonely and gorgeous for free back on the other side of the country.

The Professor and Mary Ann abandon their seats at the other end of the bar, and someone sidles up to take their place.

"Anything?" the much-put-upon bartender asks.

"Not yet," Orin says. "I'm waiting for someone."

Sweet Jesus, the con hasn't fucking started. How much more awkward can it get?

"No, you're not," Laura says, a little ways behind him. "If I'm talking to the right person."

Why do I tempt fate like this? Of *course* it can get more awkward. God, I hope my hoodie is enough to mask my face. Maybe I look like I'm cosplaying someone from Assassin's Creed and they won't look twice.

"I think you are," Orin says. He stands up to shake her hand. In all these years, I'd forgotten how tall he was. And how beardy. Maybe someone will assume *he's* cosplaying hipster Sandor Clegane. And Laura—

—*Oh shit she's hot* doesn't even begin to describe it. She's curvy and confident and that studded snapback she's wearing is a work of art, and I am in just the right position to see her unbearably generous butt as she sits on the barstool. And her smile, while she asks the bartender for a Jack and Coke. And puts down her own cash before Orin can presume, thank god.

He orders a Guinness and opens a tab, then turns back to Laura. "Everything went okay at reg?"

"Yeah, we're clear for tomorrow, 7 p.m." She takes an iPad out of her purse and props it up on the bar between them, already loading the con schedule. "It's up against one of the costume contests, the Riot panel, and the Smash Bros. tournament, so we've got competition. But it's there, in print."

Orin looks it over, smiling in the faint light of the screen. "In my experience there's not much overlap between the SSBB tournament crowd and the kind of people who'll come to a panel on diversity in gaming."

"In my experience, there *is*," she says. looking him square in the eye. "I've whupped many an ass as Princess Peach."

"I concede." He's smiling too. But he seems like he's had worse jetlag than I have. Then again, I have a shiner from yesterday and I'm skulking at a bar alone, listening to my it's-*still*-complicated and the subject-of-my-dubiously-requited-affection meet for the first time, so I'm probably no prize for the eyes either. "Are we still working from the same PowerPoint?" Orin goes on.

"Sort of. Bobby's flight got delayed out of Vancouver, so they might not be here until late tomorrow. We can divide up some of their talking points between the four of us, or just drop them for more Q&A at the end."

"Is that the kind of bridge we cross when we come to it?"

"Unfortunately, no." The bartender sets their drinks down, and she thanks him, but edges the Jack and Coke a fair bit farther from the iPad. "In fact, it might be a good idea for you to meet the others anyway. We can take this upstairs."

I cannot even begin to describe how relieved I am that she says those words—the words that most people use as an opportunity to vamp it up when they're reading sides—as neutrally as possible. It's a hotel. Everything is upstairs. That she's inviting him upstairs has nothing to do with— Oh who am I kidding? I am jealous as fuck right now. Jealous that it's easy to ask, and jealous that it's him she's asking.

She clarifies before he can say yes, "Jahata's got a room party going. If we don't pry her away from it before everyone else shows up, she won't be much good for talking."

"Right. I'm not sure how good I'll be with room party crowds at the moment," Orin admits. "Let me give you my number so you can check in with her first—and so I can go upstairs and get my laptop, sorry—and then we can meet back down here? Or just in the lobby?"

I shouldn't be so elated to hear him turn her down.

"I'm fine with that," Laura says, then takes a sip of her drink through the tiny red straws. "If you want to come by later when the crowd's thinned out, that's cool too. Maybe then we *won't* immediately Falcon Punch you into orbit."

He laughs. "Sounds like a plan." He raises his Guinness to toast.

She clinks her glass on his. "To keeping the conversation going."

"In the face of greater odds than a more generous god would have allowed," Orin agrees, and then they both drink.

"Your number, right" she says, and sets the glass back down to fish her phone out of her purse. "And—just checking—you're not here alone, are you? I mean, after everything online?"

"Alas, yes." He sighs, still holding on to his pint. "Honestly, it's better that I'm rooming alone, and the hotel staff made sure my room door is in a clear line of sight to the security cameras. But there's not much else they can do. The con staff said they'd make sure that panel security was good, but I'm fairly certain that really means *extant*."

She puts the phone down in front of him, and I can't quite see from around the tablet and the glasses, but I think she just patted his hand. "I'm sorry you have to deal with this. I know what it's like."

"Honestly, I'm glad it's happening to me and not Fatiguee."

Laura tilts her head, curls shifting like a dark stormcloud. "Is she here too?"

I should leave. I picked up the exit cue a scene ago, and this one's even louder, even clearer.

"I don't know," Orin sighs. "She went off the grid a few days ago. I think she's screening everyone's calls, not only mine. I wish she'd let me help her."

"You are," Laura says, and this time she definitely pats his arm. "You're fighting for her where she doesn't feel safe."

"Is it still fighting if she would rather I give up?"

"You know, a friend of mine asked me the same thing the other day. If it's still the same fight." Oh shit, she means me. Daphnis. Bannedict. Whichever. "And I said I think it is. If she trusts you to carry the banner, we can still fight."

"I hope she does, then." Orin finishes thumbing his number into her phone, then takes another gulp of beer.

I have exactly enough cash to settle my tab here. I won't ask for change. I don't want to worry about giving the bartender my card, just want to pull the hood up and get out and—

"Talk to her," Laura says. "If she lets you. And if she doesn't, this fight's about you too. Not in the same way, but it is."

"I'll take that under advisement," he says, smiling tightly, and signals the bartender.

Years of dance classes have enabled me to make a stealthy, silent exit from many a situation. This one's no different. But I still find it hard to go, if only because I can't take my eyes off either of them even after I make it out to the lobby.

CHAPTER EIGHTEEN

Alain is no longer an eight-foot-tall bunny girl, but I think she's still Ivy. She's commandeered the bathroom and is fighting an angular silver and blue wig into place, and doesn't look away from the mirror until I'm already the whole way in. "Everything okay?"

I flash my badge. "I got my shit from SummerStorm, and the meeting's on Sunday afternoon. How'd your shoot go?"

"We got kicked off the roof, but Lexi got a few good shots before that. So we finished the shoot up at the hotel across the street. They've got better gardens." Apparently satisfied with the wig itself, she starts clipping in a prissy cat-ear tiara covered in spikes and rhinestones. "And my eyebrow game is so on right now that there's no way in hell I'm wasting this face. Lexi invited me to a thing in room 542. You want in?"

"Sure." I've got nothing better to do, and Jackie's still out with her harem of fangirls. Besides, there are few things more pathetic than sitting around a hotel room alone. Orin must be doing that to avoid the crowds. I know he said it's not my fault, but it still feels terrible to be responsible—

"Earth to Daphnis," Ivy says, twirling her fingers in front of my face. "Come in, Daphnis."

"I said 'sure,'" I clarify, and try not to grimace.

Ivy pouts. "What, too much?"

"No, I promise it's not you." I give her the short form of what just happened with Laura and Orin downstairs while Ivy changes her lipstick and trades out her fuzzy slippers for spiky ankle boots. She looks like she's going to an underground club in Seoul, not a room party in Seattle, but I'm in no place to judge. And it's hot, so. We must make an interesting pair: enormous Algerian glamazon and average-sized whatever-I-am with a nerd shirt and only a trendy haircut to set me apart from the faceless masses.

It doesn't count as judging if I judge me, not her.

Wait. There's something there. There's something potentially earth-shattering there, lurking in the back of my head with all the spiders and weasels.

But then Ivy is leading me out the door, and we're in the elevator, and there are two people in it dressed as rainbow squids with water guns, and I've got a room full of people I've never met to impress.

Room 542, and adjoining room 544, is the site of even more rainbow squids than we encountered in the elevator. Both televisions are currently rollicking with the same game, which is described to me by one of the rooms' hosts as a territory-claiming shooter. Which perhaps explains the squids, but they're spraying paint, not ink, and that's just weird.

Either way, the game's pretty awesome. I grab a decent beer out of the cooler and leave two dollars next to it to be polite, and Ivy and I cut in on one of the screens when that squid battle is done.

Ivy's friend and photographer Lexi is wiping the floor with anyone who signs on, so I'm not too concerned about coming in third place as long as I don't come in last. Ivy, less lucky in shooters than in makeup skills, demurs with characteristic grace and wanders off in search of more beer, but I stick around for another two games and get a much better hang on the controls. The crowd may shift, but it stays at about the same density—maybe twenty, twenty-five people crammed in the suite—and even if security shows up, we're just drinking and playing video games. Which is likely much tamer behavior than security's ever dealt with.

Orin said something about cameras in the halls. They've probably got a handle on this.

Lexi still wins round three, but I improve my rank enough to yield my spot to the next person without feeling like a complete loser.

"Thanks," Laura says as she reaches for my controller.

And then she recognizes me.

"Daphnis?"

"Hey," I manage. I could go on and on about how adorable she is, but I've done that already. Instead I notice, because we're so close I can't help it, "Your eyes are two different colors."

Open mouth, insert squid.

But she laughs, and grins, and playfully adjusts her glasses. "Yeah. Many a romance novel has been invoked when people first clock these."

"I can see why." I offer up my hand—oh shit, I still have the controller in it—but she closes her hand around my fist and shakes it anyway.

"It's really good to see you," she says.

"Yeah, I've been—" Orin already said Fatiguee was *off the grid*, so I thankfully catch myself in time, "—dealing with my agent. He said we could go in a new direction after that last audition didn't work out."

"That's a relief." She plops down on the bed next to me, nudging someone else's sweatshirt aside. "I didn't know you know Lexi and Jahata."

"I don't," I admit. "My roommate did a photoshoot with Lexi."

"Sweet, which one?"

I get the feeling Ivy would rather make the introduction herself, so I just cast about the room and try to point her out. She's perched on the edge of the dresser, chatting, looking over presumably Lexi's shoulder as she scrolls through her camera's display.

"Definitely introduce me," Laura says, and takes my hand again. This time, I drop the controller. No exaggeration—I just got a static shock straight from her touch to my heart. Could be the hotel comforter, could be desperation. "C'mon!"

What can I say? I'm a sucker when a hot girl bosses me around.

In those shoes, Ivy towers over nearly everyone in the room, so she definitely spots us on our way over. "I think I know what's going on," she says, rolling back her shoulders and putting on a true cat smile. "Daphnis, is this—"

I nod. "Laura, this is my roommate and fellow Musketqueer," I offer, and Ivy takes care of the rest.

Which means tilting forward to flaunt her contoured cleavage and the trademark "tipsy curtsey" victory pose. "Ivy LeVine, too fine to prune."

If I thought Laura was beautiful when she smiles, it's nothing compared to her when she busts a gut laughing. "You definitely are," she manages when she comes back up for air. Then, softer, she checks in: "Female pronouns?"

She never asked mine. Wait, no. Yes, she did, months ago. Or did she? Or did I just introduce myself as what I am? Why am I thinking about this *now*, of all times, when she's right here and we could be talking about anything but this bullshit in my head?

Ivy answers, "'She' when I'm tucked, 'he' when I'm not. Alain and Ivy are two separate people."

"Great," she says, tapping her temple, "I'll file that away. Your accent isn't as thick as Daphnis's—have you been in the states longer?"

"A little; since I was twelve." And then Ivy launches into a somewhat-in-character, somewhat-out story about our first meeting, which I'd be one hundred percent okay to listen to if I hadn't just spotted the figurative elephant in the room.

Or the bull in the china shop.

Orin is framed in the doorway, clearly looking for someone he recognizes. That someone definitely can't be me. I try to turn aside, make sure my face isn't reflected in the mirrored closet or the television screen, and then it occurs to me: he's here to see Laura. This is the party she invited him to. And I'm standing *right next to her* and can't get out without her noticing.

Ivy goes on, "So there's this kid, walking in halfway through the year, all mousy and—"

"Ivy," I interrupt, "I think that one's more your type." And then I add, in French, just to make sure she gets my meaning, "And *really not mine*, so if you could catch him first?"

Ivy follows where I cock my head, and definitely recognizes that I'm indicating Orin. It's harder to read her face under all the makeup, but there's no mistaking the mischievous glint I've known in *Alain's* eyes for all these years. That is the *I fervently hope he gets my Ultimate Odyssey jokes* glint. The *and even if he doesn't, I'm gonna keep making them* glint. And the *someone is offering me a dollar if I lip-synch in his general direction and that'll turn into a twenty if I whisper in his ear that I like handcuffs* glint.

She leans down and air-kisses me over the cheek, right under the bruise. "All for one."

"One for all," I countersign. I'll bet I'm no longer owed all the drinks for that fiasco yesterday.

Ivy gives an air-kiss to Laura as well and says, "Forgive me, I think there's someone I need to intercept. I'll be right back." And then she saunters off in Orin's direction, and I can trust Ivy to occupy someone's attention completely.

At the precise same time, Laura gets a text, and points up to excuse herself and read it. I can slip away, no problem, and take advantage of the door between the rooms to exit through 544 instead of 542.

Once I'm out in the hall, it's not too far to the elevator. That went much better than I expected it to—the party was fine until Orin got there, and Laura is so magnetic and no-nonsense that if Orin hadn't shown up, I'd have stayed all night. It sucks that we were cut short, but by the time I get to the elevator I've resigned myself to seeing her at the panel tomorrow, and then, maybe, we can keep talking and work some of this out.

"Daphnis!" she calls, "Glad I caught you."

Or we could talk now. Now's good.

"Sorry, I didn't mean to abandon you," she says, jogging over and stopping right by the elevator call button.

"You didn't." This is, again, one hundred percent truth. "It's okay, it just got crowded in there, that's all."

"Yeah, it's hard to have a conversation at a party. And I've got panel stuff I need to take care of, so I was wondering—"

Why is it that whenever something potentially good happens, something three times as bad fucks it up?

"—you know that Diversity in Games panel I'm running? It's tomorrow night, and one of the other panelists is stuck in Vancouver and might not make it in time. I was wondering if you might want to take their slot. Or maybe go over what you've experienced first with just us, if you don't want to get up and talk about it in front of everyone. I thought your experiences might be similar, so. If you're interested."

"I—" I'm interested all right. It's still a loaded term. And any excuse to talk with her, the better. But not at the panel. Not with Orin there next to her, knowing how much I've lied to both of them. "I'm not sure. But I'd love to keep talking to you."

The elevator dings and opens, and we both stand aside.

"That's fine," she says. "Here, let me give you my number so we can check in before the panel."

"What panel?" a vaguely familiar voice asks, as the elevator shuts behind him.

Laura and I both look up, and I could not have staged this more awkwardly. It's Mal Harding again, *Monsieur Publicité*, eyebrow piqued to the brim of his trilby.

"The Diversity in Games panel, tomorrow at seven," Laura answers, pitch-perfect. "It's mostly about the climate of harassment these last few weeks. And years."

Harding shakes his head. "There's no such panel."

One moment, I'm blinking at Laura, as incredulous as she is; the next, she's phased into the kind of stance I'm sure she's used in law school, dubious but composed and rooted to the floor. "I have proof on my phone that the panel was approved, and it's on my schedule that I received at panelist registration."

"It might be on your schedule, but I just got back from con ops and it's not on the master record or printed in the program. It must have been cut in the last couple of days." Harding doesn't look particularly apologetic, but he's not sniveling either, like he was for me downstairs. "It might have been up against too many important things."

"Important," Laura repeats. "Really. Some people came to this con specifically for this panel."

Harding scoffs through his nose. "That's ridiculous. Who comes to a gaming convention to talk about things that have nothing to do with gaming? That's probably why the panel got cut."

Laura meets him brow for brow. "'The panel got cut,' or 'you cut the panel'?"

Harding shrugs, then tips his hat and starts walking off. "I'm sure you'll find something else to do," he says, heading down the opposite hall from the room party, and disappears around a corner.

By the time Laura has her phone out, he's gone; in another minute she's searched through the schedule file, and come up with nothing.

"He's right," she whispers, incredulous. "It's gone. That makes no sense. I checked in for it this afternoon. Who *was* that guy?"

"SummerStorm publicity," I answer, because she should know.

"Mal Harding," she half asks. "The one who sent Fatiguee that email."

Yes. "I think so," I lie instead. "I heard it was an intern." Now I'm not so sure.

But I'm crystal clear on one thing: it's all my fault.

CHAPTER NINETEEN

I spend the remainder of the night, once I get back to our hotel room, staring at Laura's phone number in my contacts. At least I've got something good, still, though it's going to get worse and worse if she finds out I'm the reason her panel got cut. Well. The reason *Harding cut her panel*. The reason beside Harding being an ambulatory piece of shit, at any rate. But I got her number. She doesn't hate me. Yet.

Jackie comes in around 1 a.m., Alain at one thirty, and by the time Alain's out of his makeup Jackie is out like a light. I wonder if she sleeps better at cons.

I clearly don't.

The combination of Alain fighting with the hair dryer and the smell of pancakes wakes me up at eight thirty. Good lord above, Jackie ordered room service. As long as she's paying for the room, I won't stop her, but it seems insanely extravagant. Alain isn't getting into costume until later and has to go pick up his badge anyway, so he scarfs down some pancakes and sausage and says he'll text me when he gets through the line so I don't have to wait with him. And Jackie's panels are mostly at night, because they're ostensibly not family friendly, but the one that isn't is in only two hours so she's going to hook up with her harem before then.

No panels I'm interested in until one thirty; I can just take in the sights until then. I haven't been to a con in a couple of years, and it's pretty easy to forget how much I just missed the *environment* of them: thousands of people, every single one a huge fucking nerd but all wildly different, congregating in celebration and driving hotel staff to early graves. I get an enormous coffee and hang around in one of the alcoves that overlook the con center lobby, just watching all the exquisite chaos. Friends reunite after months or years apart, groups and individuals pose in their elaborate costumes for swarms of photographers, teenagers parade with their in-jokes and exuberance and leave their chaperones bewildered in the dust. A mock-fight between a scarily realistic Transformer and a ludicrously oversized Pikachu breaks out in the entrance, and a circle of people document the indignity for future generations. Silly robot, Steel types are always weak to Electric.

After a quick detour to the bathroom—gender-neutral, in the hotel Starbucks—a cadre of Elegant Gothic Lolitas has stolen my seat, so I venture forth with a couple of hours to kill. The line for the dealers' room is ridiculous, so I hit up Artist Alley first. There's the usual spread of fanart of variable quality and style, plus jewelry and chain mail accessories, shot glasses with various iconography (Alain already owns a full set of the Ultimate Odyssey ones, in numerical order), hand-knit Hogwarts scarves and Firefly hats, and buttons with slogans and chibis from everything that's been popular ever. Since I don't have much to spend, I feel terrible lingering at any table for long, lest I get someone's hopes up. But there's one T-shirt stand with a few *Eternal Reign* memes in bombastic colors: *Don't Fuck With Doctor Conesto* in the style of those old Keep Calm and Carry On shirts, *My Other Ride Is a Kharthi Galleon* (also available as a bumper sticker, and probably better-suited to that), and one with *Navigators Find the Sweet Spot* in bright magenta. They're $20 each. Maybe they'll cost less on Sunday. Or maybe I could buy one now, since Jackie seems to be taking care of breakfast—

Alain texts me and saves me from taking advantage of Jackie's hospitality. He's out of the registration line (it only took two hours, that's impressive) and he's still got time to kill before he has to go upstairs and get in drag. Meet him at the East Versus West RPGs panel? Sure, it's not far. I hadn't planned on going—those panels usually devolve into either side of the debate claiming moral superiority, and there's only so much of that I can take right now—but if Alain's there, we can always be our own entertainment.

It turns out to be a well-attended panel, if the line outside the ballroom is any indication. Alain is holding a spot for me about fifty bodies in and waves me over. Considering what he's wearing, I have to wonder if people think he's cosplaying some J-rock idol or BL manga hero.

After we catch up on the con so far—I show him the video I took of the Transformer/Pikachu fight, I knew he'd want to see it—he leans down and whispers, "By the way, is everything okay? About last night, I mean."

"Yeah, it's fine. I just didn't want to talk to Orin yet."

"Yeah, he can talk a *lot*," Alain agrees. Only a *little* bit lewdly.

"Wait. What?"

Alain waves his hands in front of himself defensively, but keeps smirking. "We didn't do anything. He just kept my ear until Laura came back and relieved me. Did you know he recognized my costume from yesterday? And me from the costume? You never told me he played for my team too."

"Yeah, sometimes," I manage, "assuming you mean console games and not cocksucking."

He cackles, and the con staff starts ushering the line forward, so we file in. "Well, whether he'll blow me or not, he's got my number. And he wants to see me in my Lydia masterpiece later. Do you think he'll come to the cosplay drag show?"

"I have no idea." We find seats in the panel room, and I'm forced to contemplate the image of Orin at a drag show, cosplay or otherwise. Nope. Not that beardy white knight. Maybe he could be persuaded to make an anthropological assessment of the place and get into a heated argument with the emcee about contest rules. But no, I can't really picture it.

There are surprisingly few technical difficulties for this panel, or maybe the interface has just gotten smarter. Three panelists—all men—have congregated at the table on the dais, surrounded by pitchers of water and their laptops. Their PowerPoint display flashes onto a projection screen off to the side: an evocative animated gif pits three cartoonified Ultimate Odyssey heroes against three Bioware ones in the style of a fighting game, with the flashing caption *East vs. West: Battle of the RPGs*.

"This already looks competent," I mutter.

Alain agrees, and messes around with his phone to text the same to one of his UO friends who may also be in the audience.

The panel gets started with a couple of taps on the mic, and alternate cheers and polite applause from the two hundred or so people in the audience. The shortest of the panelists calls everyone to order in the manner of a petty dictator, with a big smug smile and a five-o'clock shadow even though it's only noon.

"All right, so let's make sure you know who we are," he says, and the opening animation shifts to a static screen with all their names and Twitter handles. "Our fourth says he's on his way—something about a smoke bomb in the video game room, don't ask me—so I'll let him cover that when he gets here. But I think I can pick up his slack for now."

Same cheers, same applause.

"So," the short one says, "let's let my esteemed opponents introduce themselves first:"

The man on my far right waves. "Hi, I'm Justin Buonafonte. I write for UOO and *Kotaku*, and I've been a connoisseur of JRPGs for about twenty years. I work as a localizer for Shueisha USA, and I own versions of *Ultimate Odyssey IV* on four different platforms, so I guess you know what side I'm on."

Next to me, Alain murmurs in French, "He banned me on the forums three times when I was a teenager."

I snicker. "I remember that."

The man in the middle, much reedier than Justin, with lanky black hair, waves at the audience. "Hey, everyone, I'm Dan Jameson. I'm the lead writer and narrator on Stat Boost—" pause for cheers "—which, for those of you who don't know, is one of the biggest game education platforms on YouTube. I give lectures on game design and development at colleges all around the world, and I'm a huge fan of Western RPGs too, but I'm fighting for Team East today because I think the way Japan has contributed to the development of the medium is extremely important. I'm also in charge of recording this entire panel as a podcast, so I'll basically be acting as the moderator."

The short one, who was the first to speak, picks up where Dan left off. "And I'm Neal Merino. I'm the MMO correspondent for Jongleur, the maintainer of the *Eternal Reign* subreddit, and the writer and talent on both the English and Spanish iterations of *No Mercy*."

The applause is briefly staggered, then deafening. I clap with everyone else, just not as loudly. I've probably read Neal's articles on Jongleur—I'll have to check—and I've definitely seen a few webisodes of *No Mercy*, which takes pride in ripping new critical holes in MMO missions and expansions. It's not my taste, but that must be why his voice is so familiar. And if he's an *ER* player, I might have run across him at some point.

Neal goes on, "And, if I'm being frank, I think JRPGs have lost whatever magic they had in the first place and have descended into a cesspit of visual spectacle at the expense of innovative gameplay, and that there hasn't been a viable alternative to the turn-based battle system out of the East in the last ten years."

The other panelists laugh. "Wow, man," says Justin, "tell us how you really feel."

Neal preens. "I will, since my debate partner isn't here to slag on everything that doesn't uphold his ideal of a PC Master Race."

The panel begins in earnest, with the PowerPoint shaping the direction of the debate. They assume that everyone here knows the history of the genres, which is good, because I at least have a general overview, and launch into a spirited discussion of combat systems. It's obvious that they've all met before this to plan, so that they don't just yell at each other, which makes the panel rather entertaining compared to the others, but a little staged and inorganic. My attention drifts phone-ward a couple of times at the start, but their positions cut through my brain haze and become abundantly clear as it goes: Justin thinks that Western RPGs, including MMOs, owe everything they have to Japan and should pay their respects, Dan is being all academic about the anthropological reasons that each country would develop games a certain way and sounds like he's talked about this before, in abundance, without interruption; and Neal couldn't give two shits about games with narrative content and says that no mass-market Japanese game puts the emphasis on a gameplay experience and they're getting less and less gamelike as the years go on.

"I have to tell you," Neal says, when we get to slide three, "when I sit down at a computer or a console, I'm not looking for a story. I'm not there for a visual experience. I'm not there for narrative. If I wanted narrative, I'd read a book, and if I wanted visuals I'd watch TV. When I play a game, I'm looking to match myself and my skills against another person, whether that person is playing at the same time as me, or whether the person wrote a story-mode game beforehand and expects me to solve it. Just because I'm playing a role doesn't mean I want to follow someone else's script. JRPGs uniformly start with a story they already expect me to tell, and reward me for good play with the next installment of something they already wrote, regardless of how I perform. Western RPGs, including MMOs, put much more of an emphasis on how the players can actually affect the game world, and since the way the players affect the world is through *playing*, they have to put gameplay at the top of their priorities. JRPGs are stories that want to be told, so they make themselves as easy and breakable as possible. Western RPGs fight back."

Alain doesn't clap with everyone else for that one, and raises his hand once the applause is done.

"Can we take a question?" Dan asks Neal, who nods and points at Alain.

"Yes?"

Alain stands up and looks Neal square in the eyes. "You said you mostly play MMOs—are you open to console JRPGs? 'Cause I know a few with systems that will keep you up at night."

Neal tilts up his chin and laughs. "I already know about Kilosei. They've been dumbing the system down since *Anahata*, and if I recall correctly the Survivor series hasn't put out a game since 2005. Furthermore, just because the enemies take forever to fall doesn't mean they can't be beaten over and over the same way once you crack the pattern."

"I wasn't talking about Kilosei," Alain says. "Though you're right, that did kick my ass. I was talking about *Jitlandia Tactics II*."

"The question of whether tactical RPGs are still RPGs for purposes of this debate aside, the battle system for Jitlandia was outsourced to a Canadian company and implemented in the East. I'll make sure the source for that is attached to the podcast version of this panel so you can find it afterward if Google doesn't turn anything up."

"And Jitlandia's shit, Ivy," Ivan calls from the ballroom door. "Sorry I'm late, Krozin."

"It's cool," Neal says.

"It's *Alain*, asshole," Alain says.

"*Merde*," I say, because *of course Ivan is here* and *of course Neal is Krozin*, because *this is my ridiculous fucking life.*

"Krozin! That's her!" Ivan yells. "That's Fatiguee!"

Neal—*Krozin*—curses into the microphone in Spanish.

There is only one option, and that option is run like hell, so I bolt for the end of the row. I will not sit here and let this panel become about me, and I *know* that Ivan is going to start shit. Thank god this is a ballroom and there's more than one way out. Ivan's already headed toward me down one of the aisles; I take off down the other, and ignore all the shouting from the panelists and the general chaos of the crowd. I manage to get to a set of doors and shove through—and then I'm not the only one trying to leave. Not the only one running. And once I get into the halls it's an out-and-out clusterfuck.

Hey, if anyone tries to rag on me for running in the halls, I can always plead that I don't speak English. But right now I'm more concerned with losing the trail. I don't know where I'm going, just that I have to fight to get there. I skid past a Marvel Comics photoshoot, nearly crash into a water cooler, and duck behind a placard to catch my breath. At least one person asks if I'm okay, and another is trying to tape this on her phone, so no. No rest. No time. I'm *screwed.*

"You lying little bitch," Ivan mutters to himself as he passes by, Krozin and five others on his heels. "You'll pay for this."

"Ivan, stop." Wow, Neal, Krozin, whichever, is even shorter than I expected. He must be barely Jackie's size, but muscled like a fencer. "We have a *panel* to run. Can't we deal with this later?"

"You're the one who started this, Krozin. I know she came this way—"

"Fatiguee's an in-game problem. We can deal with her in-game. In the real world we've got two hundred people waiting for you to tell them why JRPGs are shit, and if you don't do it, they're gonna revoke your badge."

"But you're—"

"I'm chasing you, not her. You're already late."

Ivan groans. "Fine. But I'm ripping her a new one if I see her later. Bitch threw my phone into the sewer back in New York."

"That's your business, not mine. I only frag her characters, not her." Krozin claps a hand on Ivan's arm and turns him around. "Let's go."

I wait for them to be far enough away, and make sure no one else is searching for me, before I start breathing again. My throat is searing, but I'm alive. And here. And not going back to that panel, so I'd better tell Alain I'm safe. I get out my phone while I'm still down here, start texting him, *I'm okay*.

It's a half truth, like everything else I say.

Almost as soon as I get the text out, a huge hand comes down on my shoulder. "Are you oka— *Daphne?*"

Shit. Orin. Of all the times. But I can't help tilting up, and I have nowhere to go, and there he is, looming over me like the angel he wishes he could be.

"I'm so sorry," he says, and god, he looks like I feel, except enormous. "If you want me to go, I'll go. I just want you to be okay. I know you probably don't want to talk to me, but—"

"Orin, now is not the time." It's not all I want to say, but it's all I've got, and as long as I'm curled up pathetic down here, if I let out any of the rest, it'll be a goddamn scene. "Don't go back to that panel. You were there, weren't you? That's how you found me."

He at least has the grace to look sheepish. "Yeah. I was there. I knew Neal is Krozin, and I was going to call him out."

"Please, just don't. Don't fight anymore."

"But if I don't—"

"I'm *sick of it*." Okay, this *is* going to be a scene. "Orin, I'm *tired*. And this isn't like fighting in-game. You can't make a new character and start over. I've been trying, and I can't. I am what they say I am, and that's it, and even if you could win, I wouldn't be worth fighting for!"

He kneels down to hug me, and it is the last thing in the world I want.

Can I still call it a tactical retreat if I'm literally just running away?

CHAPTER TWENTY

aura gives me her room number when I text. It turns out that 544 was hers to begin with, so here I am, outside last night's squid nexus, sitting with my back to the door and quickly running out of power on my phone. I'm missing the one thirty panel I meant to go to, but hey. I'm not even paying to be at this con. Maybe I'm only in Seattle to take up space.

"I heard about Krozin's panel," Laura says when she gets here. Instead of kneeling down, she offers me a hand and helps me up. "That would upset anyone with sense."

"I think Ivan's very existence is upsetting," I agree. "Sorry we have to talk at a time like this."

"Any time's good." She shrugs, smiles, and scans her room key to let us both in. "It's called a convention for a reason. What's it for, if not convening? Come in."

That's just the kind of joke I need to hear, though laughing doesn't come easily, and I follow her in. Now that the room isn't wall-to-wall people, it looks pretty much like ours, minus the heaps of Alain's cosplay materials and wigs on every lamp. She sits on the edge of one of the double beds, and pats the space next to her. So I sit.

"So is it true?" Laura asks, then clarifies, "Are you Fatiguee's player?"

I nod. "That obvious, huh?"

"Unfortunately, no." But she smiles, rubs her nose. "I'm glad you're comfortable telling me. To be fair, I suspected that might be the case when you were avoiding Orin yesterday, but I still wasn't sure."

"I'd rather have told you myself from the start. I owe you an enormous apology."

"Well, now you don't." She covers my hand with hers, runs her thumb across my knuckles. "That sounded like an apology to me. But you don't have to be sorry for doing what you had to do to feel safe. I promise, this doesn't change much."

"Much?"

"It makes me even *more* disappointed that there's not going to be a panel for us." Her smile fades at the edges, right up to her mismatched eyes. "If you were here, we'd be able to present proof positive of the problem. But they're not letting us speak."

"Have you brought it up with ops?"

"It's like Harding said. Ops told me the panel was cut two days ago, before they finalized the programs. And they won't reinstate it." She sighs, fidgets with her glasses, and the bed creaks. "How they can cut it at the last minute is . . . well, not beyond me, I understand it perfectly. It's just the same hateful rhetoric they've been up to for years."

"It's a shame we can't do a guerilla panel," I wonder aloud.

". . . a guerilla panel?"

"Like guerilla theater," I say. "Sprung up and advertised where they can't stop us but still on convention grounds. If they let photoshoots go unscheduled, why not a panel?"

"Because of the fire codes," Laura points out. "But I think you're on to something."

"Maybe. I mean, I know how to advertise it. Jackie's panels were all approved, and she's got an enormous following, so we could start with her if we could figure out a place."

"Well we can't do it here if the rooms are all full." That amazing smile comes flooding back, like even her freckles are getting in on the mischief. "But we don't have to do it *here*. This isn't the only hotel in the area. And if we hold it at a different hotel, the convention isn't liable, and can't legally stop us." She flings her arms around me and cheers. "Daphnis, you're a genius!"

I barely croak out, "It was your idea—" before she kisses me.

It's quick and sudden, but definite lip-to-lip contact, and it shuts me up so that when she pulls away to take this to the internet, I have nothing to say. She kissed me. She called me Daphnis and she still kissed me. And now she's looking up pricing on hotel conference rooms at the other buildings on this street, and telling me to take notes, and everything just falls right into place. She draws up a plan, and estimates attendance, and double-checks the convention rules to make sure they don't have some kind of exclusivity clause in them, which they don't. And I help. It's better than being downstairs at some other panel: it's the easy pattern we fell into online. Easier than acting. Easier than Orin.

After she sends out an email enquiry, she kisses me again, and this time, we don't stop for I don't know how long.

Okay. I still love conventions. Even if I wind up chased down the hall by angry video game nerds once in a while, there are moments like this. Moments like falling into bed with a gorgeous, brilliant lady who can still joke about puzzle quests while she's telling me to unhook her bra. Moments like her glasses fogging up a little while we're kissing, but her saying it's okay, she wants to keep them on. She's soft and full all over, and she warns me to be careful with her hair, so I tell her she can keep my hands out of the way. She does. She accepts me immediately, takes me in stride, holds my wrists to the mattress and gives me a framework in which to improvise.

She accepts everything she finds.

She runs her hands over my binder, knows exactly what it is, and pinches me through it hard enough that I can feel it on the other side. I'm not sure I'd mind taking it off just to feel her hands on my skin, but we can worry about that later. She has me where she wants me, and I am a hundred percent on board. Her tongue trails a stripe up my neck, and she says she loves my haircut, it's fuzzy, and I'm still laughing when she slips a hand down the front of my jeans—

And her goddamn phone rings, but hey. We can always resume. I think. I hope.

Laura picks up, muttering about who calls anymore when there's email, "Hello? . . . Yes, this is she . . . . No, we're not affiliated with the convention, just attending it. In the interest of full disclosure, this is because they cancelled a panel with an expected attendance of over two hundred people, and there's still a great deal of— Oh, good. That should be fine." She mouths at me, *Pen?*

I scramble off the bed and grab a pen and paper from the pile of stuff on the desk, half of which seems to be soft drinks and the other half peanut butter sandwich fixings.

By the time I get back to her, she's grinning ear to ear. "That's entirely reasonable. When do you need the deposit? . . . That may not be possible. Will you give us until midnight? . . . All right. Thank you. Yes, you can put the hold under my name. Thank you again. Can I have your name, please?" She writes it, and the number, down on the pad and ends the call.

"We're in?" I guess.

"If we can get three thousand dollars by midnight to pay for the room."

I nod. "My laptop's downstairs—I can set up the microdonations and get Jackie on board. And she can announce it at her panel tonight, so that should get us what we need."

"Great. I'll draft up a release and get the others to spread it around. You don't mind that I still want Orin to talk?"

"It's fine," I say. "I don't think I'm ready to talk anyway, and he's got a lot to say."

She's already on her way to her tablet and whips out the keyboard to go with it. "I'm— Wow, I just realized that this looks like I'm telling you to get out. I'm sorry."

"It doesn't. That was— I mean." Words suck. "This is more important. It's what you came to the con to do. There's time for, um, anything else. Later. If you want to."

To answer my question, she pushes back from the desk, crosses to me, and kisses me again. "I do if you do," she says, so close to me I can see the smudges in her lipstick.

I do doesn't even begin to say it, but I say it anyway.

Jackie texts that she'll meet me back at the room. Also that she's told Alain I'm okay, and he's already there getting ready. I'll tell them the good news in person, since it's pretty much inextricable from everything else, but—

Orin's waiting at the door, like I was for Laura.

Great. Just great.

CHAPTER TWENTY-ONE

I really hope Alain's phone is in reach of whatever the hell he's doing in there, because it's about to explode with texts.

Alain

Come in Alain

Orin is waiting outside but I need to get in to talk to Jackie when she gets here

Can you run a diversion

Or maybe just call security on him I don't know

I stay out of sight behind a convenient potted plant around the corner. I can see him if I try and— Right, I should turn off the ringer for when Alain texts back.

Gladly

Now you definitely owe me show attendance

He's about to get a preview

I don't get time to thank him, because the door swings open, with enough force to rustle Orin's beard, and we are all graced with a vision in lime green.

There's the enormous green wig festooned with feathers and jewels, the bright glittering makeup, the sequined and spangled leotard covered in silver whorls and gold stars, thigh-high boots with at least six different kinds of trim, and yards upon yards of patterned chiffon trailing off her arms. I'm not sure if it's gorgeous or atrocious, but I guess that's fashion for you. Ivy walked right out of someone's D&D campaign art from the mid-1990s after Liberace got hold of her and sent her down a Paris runway.

And she's carrying a coiled gold whip, like Wonder Woman's lasso. Orin's jaw just about hits the floor.

"You're not welcome in Nebelton," Ivy says, affecting an absolutely perfect imperiousness and, thanks to her heels, able to look even Orin square in the eyes.

It takes two slow breaths for Orin to pant out, "You have my express permission to burn me down instead."

Well, that's definitely a diversion.

"I might take you up on that," Ivy trills, then grabs Orin by the collar and starts leading him down the hall, away from the room. "After I report you to your superior officers for being underdressed."

"I thought you were about to say *over*dressed."

"Certainly not! A knight needs his shining armor, otherwise that's a misnomer. I can't have my escort accoutered so shabbily that my magnificence *completely* outshines him. Lucky for you, I know where we can borrow a white cape in your size."

"Actually, I was waiting so I could apologize to Daphne—"

"Daph*nis*," Ivy corrects, whirling around on one heel and putting a finger right up against Orin's nose, "doesn't feel comfortable talking to you and doesn't desire your protection. I, on the other hand, would very much appreciate someone carrying my bags and making sure I don't trip on my tassels. Let it go until they come to you, and until then, attach yourself to a party that needs a paladin. Namely, me."

In the distance, an elevator dings, and Orin glances over his shoulder. I'm in his line of sight, and I know he sees me.

It feels like the first time. The same heart in my throat and the same relief, like a knot uncoiling under the necessary pressure. When I met him three years ago, I knew him just by the sound of his voice, and he knew me by mine.

Words were always easier for us than touch.

Orin nods, first to me, then to Ivy. "That's fair. And if she's— they've, sorry—given you permission to talk about it, I wouldn't mind their side of the story."

It's Ivy's turn to check with me, and I give her the same single nod. And if I can't help smiling, a little, that's still less than my friends deserve.

"Sir Orin," Ivy says, without ambiguity, "I fully intend to talk your ears off. Everything else, we can leave up for discussion."

She leads him down the hall, to the elevators and the con, and maybe this part of my life is going to work out after all.

Jackie shows up after I've taken a long shower (just for the hell of it), and I walk her through what Laura and I need her to do. I set up the microtransaction platform, link it up with Laura's article, and Jackie immediately tweets them both. (And gives us our first $300, no matter how much I protest that she doesn't have to, but honestly, I'm relieved.) Jackie then insists that I tag along with her until it's time for the drag show, which gives me a much better lease on the rest of Con Friday. We hit up the dealers' room, where Jackie buys a new hat from the steampunk peddlers and ten volumes of yuri manga. Then, since we were definitely both interested in this one, we check out the geek dance workshop and take turns impressing the youngsters for an hour and a half. A couple of the girls from Jackie's harem catch up with her, well, us, at the Japanese Speech Patterns panel, and she introduces me to them with neutral pronouns, which they immediately adopt, and keep up all the way through dinner at a pub down the block. (The experience of going out drinking with six fanfic authors, some of whom are self-confessed Rotten Women and smut peddlers, may have indelibly corrupted my ears, and I don't mind in the least. In fact, I have a whole lot of reading material for the plane home. And a few new fantasies that I might want to confess to Laura when we meet again.)

Laura texts periodically with benchmark updates, which is good because Jackie has expressly forbidden me from checking Twitter on my phone so I don't stress out too much. Apparently there is some Fatiguee-bashing in the tags, and someone linked #GuerillaPanel with #EthicalReign, but that's in its favor.

We hit $3,000 at 8 p.m., and Jackie buys the table a celebratory round of shots.

Jackie's *Yes, It's Meant for Girls* panel is at ten, and Laura shows up and spends the whole time holding my hand. It is resolved that the guerilla diversity panel will take place on Sunday at 2 p.m., right up against the SummerStorm industry panel—I couldn't have planned that better myself. And then we get in line for the drag show, and wind up fumbling through a dance routine from *Chicago* while we wait, and argue about the qualitative ranking of Kander and Ebb musicals until they check our IDs at the door. Orin doesn't come, or if he does I don't see him.

The cosplay drag show is, predictably, hilarious, and I am dead certain that Ivy made a few hundred dollars between her two sets. The Lydia set, the green one, is blindingly glamorous and apparently a laugh riot to those who have played Ultimate Odyssey, which clearly a lot of people have, but Ivy's *second* set, where she completely shanks the concept of a Fake Geek Girl to the tune of *Barbie Girl*, brings down the house. Dollar bills literally rain onto the stage. I've only seen that happen to Ivy once before, back in New York.

At that point, there's not much else to do—with no more panels, the con center after-hours has devolved into random drunkenness and pajama parties—so we head to the hotel. Laura gives me a long kiss in the lobby and says she'll see me tomorrow, since we can't exactly go back together to rooms that we're sharing with other people. (But there might be time tomorrow, she says. And I agree.)

I'm already half-asleep when Alain stumbles in and gets out of drag. By the time he starts counting his tips, Jackie's out cold, and I'm well on my way.

I wake to darkness and shattering glass.

When someone manages to turn the lights on, there's a brick wrapped in paper, just inside the broken window.

It reads: *WHORE YOURSELF OUT FOR THIS, FATIGUEE.*

CHAPTER TWENTY-TWO

Fuck the hotel staff with a rake. Yes, only the one rake.

To be fair, the hotel staff already knew how they planned to deal with this. They host multiple conventions a year, after all. GeeKon isn't even the most rambunctious of the lot—Hero World Seattle holds that dubious honor—and acts of room vandalism are unfortunately so common an occurrence that there's a flowchart in the concierge's office. It goes something like this:

INCIDENT REPORTED —> Alert senior hotel staff and local authorities —> Document evidence —> Consult security cameras —> Charge and evict perpetrators

See, room vandalism almost always comes from *inside* the room. Never mind that the laws of physics alone attest that the brick had to come from *outside*. But the problem comes at item four: there are no security cameras *outside*. Only in the halls, where they expect this shit to happen.

Did I mention that we're having this conversation at five in the morning? On a Saturday? In fucking *Seattle*?

Eventually, Jackie being a small, cute, *rich* young lady comes in as handily as we can hope: realizing that there's no chance in hell of us getting completely off the hook for something we obviously didn't do, she plays the heiress card and agrees to let the hotel charge her for the two remaining nights if they'll pretend the whole thing never happened. Alain documents his own evidence, just in case, then packs up all of his cosplay and cancels his morning photoshoots, and we spend the next few hours deciding where to go instead of having fun at the con.

Orin says he'll take Ivy in. Which is good, since Orin's otherwise alone and Alain's got so much cosplay stuff that no other roommates could put up with him. Jackie's got plenty of fangirls willing to let her crash with them, and if I read her correctly, that's what she's taking care of on her phone right now. So that leaves me.

And I'm leaving.

This bullshit has gotten me chased out of conference rooms and down the streets of New York. It's thrown itself through my hotel room window and literally ruined my sleep cycle for months. It cost one of my friends his career, and both of us a game and a story we loved. And as far as I can tell, the only way to win is not to play.

So I won't play. I pack my things and book a room that I can afford at a hotel two miles away, and text an apology to Laura. And wait for a cab by the valet's lectern.

Apparently Seattle cabs aren't as ubiquitous as NYC ones. Or maybe I'm not ready to call one. I could walk. It's only two miles. And hey, if you walk on with love in your heart, you'll never walk alone—fuck *Carousel*. Of all the times, and of all the musicals, fuck *Carousel* the most. It's not going to get out of my head.

My suitcase rolls a little to the side, and Laura sits on the curb, right next to me. "Hey," she says, quiet, gentle. "Do you mind?"

I try to say it's fine, but just end up nodding. Which can be taken both ways, can't it? I need words. Words suck. "Go ahead."

She nods back, doesn't sidle closer. "Jackie tweeted about it. You know none of this is your fault, right?"

"Fault doesn't matter." A car wheels by, and I wish I didn't have to say this all in English. "Whoever's fault it is, it keeps happening. I can't win."

"It's not about winning—"

"I can't *play*." I don't mean to shout, but I definitely raised my voice, and once it's up it won't come back down. "It's just a game to them, but I'm not playing! I'm the— They're the players, I'm just code. A random encounter. An NPC."

"But you're not," Laura says. "You're real. And this is real."

"No shit."

"That's not what I meant." She sighs and fidgets with her glasses, scrapes her heels against the concrete. The sky is as gray as the sidewalk, and there's no point on the horizon. "I'm not saying you have to fight. But I *am* saying you don't have to run away."

"I hurt people by existing," I remind her, and if I look up I *know* I'll cry, and I shouldn't. "Orin lost his job. Jackie's out thousands of dollars."

"Daphnis, you're not the one that hurt them."

"No one would have come for them if it wasn't for me!"

"I'm sorry, but that's never been true."

A car passes us by, then another, and their wake sets me shuddering.

Laura shifts closer, and I don't flinch away. "They came after me too, years ago. They still do. They've gone after my friends a hundred times. If it hadn't been you, they might have just gone straight for Jackie. Or Alain. They wouldn't have had to go through you. The kinds of people who do this, who pick someone to pile on—their reasons aren't why they do it. They do it because they think it's okay. Because they think it's allowed. Sometimes even because they think it's morally right, somehow. But either way, they do it because they can. If it were just about what you think or what you wrote, they'd have kept their opinions to themselves and their friends and you'd never hear about it. And if it were *just* about you not being like them, they'd make sexist comments and leave it at that. But people who want to prove they have power are the ones who raise the stakes. After some point, the *why* and *to whom* matter less to them than winning, so they do it for themselves. I'm not saying it's not about you, but *you* are not the problem. *You* are not the reason you're getting hurt. And I wish someone had told me that sooner, so even if you'd feel safer leaving, I'm telling you before you go."

One look into her eyes, and I keel into her arms. After that, the tears just keep coming.

She holds me and lets me ride it out. And then she waits with me until the cab comes, but doesn't make me stay.

I can't get a flight back tonight: no matter how much I try, they won't change mine over, and I can't afford to eat the cost. So it looks like I'm stuck in some out-of-the-way cheap hotel while the con goes on without me. I text Alain and Jackie to let them know where I am, and Laura to thank her and tell her I'm safe but not where.

And as long as I'm alone, and refuse to pay for hotel internet (seriously, who the hell charges for that anymore?), I guess there's nothing to do but write.

Fatiguee's story needs an ending. Her counts betrayed her, and she couldn't trust her one loyal retainer, so she abandoned her realm. Her game. Her friends. The Court of Altestis, in the end, grew weary of her machinations and her fickleness, and took matters into its own hands, and whether it's a happier and safer place or not is largely irrelevant because it's the place it wants to be, based on the people who populate it. A game, in the end, is what its players want it to be, and the players of Altestis wanted Fatiguee gone. And with her, her fraught annals, lost to time, and so the seas and tides reign eternal.

I put that in blank verse and it still sounds pathetic.

But in the end, what else am I supposed to do? In a game with no oversight—like life, maudlin as that is—the best you can do is walk away from the table. But that's not winning. No one wins. You either play or don't. Enjoy it or don't.

Alain texts: *In the lobby now what room are you in*

That's strange. He said he was staying with Orin. Either way, I answer. Maybe he's just come to check up on me.

Five minutes of depression later, Alain shows up at my door with a luggage cart and a concierge, balancing all his suitcases and wigs.

"Guess what," he says, unloading one hatbox at a time. "I overstayed my welcome."

I gape and start helping. "What?"

"He didn't kick me out," Alain quickly clarifies. "I promise, he wasn't a jerk about it. We just agreed that he's been through enough this week, and your ex-paladin doesn't need a sexuality crisis on top of everything else he's dealing with."

I almost drop the wig with the rabbit ears. "Again, *what*?"

Alain sighs. "He was expecting Ivy to show up, not me. He said he figured I was trans. I told him I'm not. He said that was fine too. Then he asked which of me he'd been talking to these last couple of days and got all academic about it, and I had to give him Compartmentalization 101, which he said was impossible. So I walked out. Then he white-knighted me down the hall and tried to tell me he was still okay with me staying, and I told him that this was proof he needs to try a new tactic and clean his own fucking keep before he besieges anyone else's. *Then* he let me go."

It takes a minute for all that to sink in. That's fine, since I spend the next two laughing my ass off.

It's not immediately contagious, but Alain eventually gives up and sheepishly tips the concierge through his own building laughter. I don't often get to be the one to kick off the hijinks, so that's kind of nice, but the laughing turns into crying, at least for me. He scrambles to get the wigs out of the way before I bawl all over them, and then we're both laughing again. And that's how Jackie finds us, sprawled in a pile of wigs on a cheap hotel bed trying not to cry.

"Does the room have a DVD player?" she asks, setting down her cargo on the desk. In addition to her suitcase, she offloads, in order, a six-pack of some pretentious Seattle microbrew, a platter of sushi, a bakery box of what looks like fancy cupcakes, and *Le Chevalier D'Eon*. Apparently Japan liked her story enough to turn it into an anime.

"Even if it doesn't, I have an HDMI," Alain answers.

I don't. "But Jackie, your panels—"

"One of the others can work from my outline," she says. "I told con ops about the break-in, and they said I'll still be welcome back next year."

"But you flew all the way out here! You should enjoy the con!"

"So should you," Alain says.

Jackie nods and sits on the bed with us. "And if you can't because of this, we won't either. All for one."

Alain joins in, and they both wait for me to give the countersign. It takes two gulps of air, and forcing my heart back down from my throat, but I get the words out in the end. "And one for all."

The cuddle-pile definitely has room for one more, especially one as tiny as Jackie. It shortly thereafter degenerates into a tickle fight. This room has thin walls, so this probably sounds like a bizarre French porno to the people next door, but I couldn't care less.

Only the eel is left on the sushi platter; we've destroyed the cupcakes; the six pack was not enough for all three of us, so Alain had to make a liquor store run and now that he's back, no one is wearing pants; and honestly, this anime is pretty good. Perhaps that's all it takes, sometimes. Just having your needs met by people who care enough to meet them.

No one even brings up the con itself until Jackie gets a text from one of the harem, and has to resend the notes because the file got corrupted. But Jackie is Jackie, and once the laptop is out, it stays out, and she starts tapping away, probably writing something, while Alain checks in with me.

"Was Orin always like that?" he asks.

"Like what?"

"Like not believing that face value exists."

I laugh, but it comes out more like a sigh. "Yes. He's always been like that. There's always a deeper meaning, a second level. It's part of why we don't work."

"Sometimes a cigar is just a cigar?" Alain jokes, switching to English.

I elbow him in the hip. "It's bigger than a cigar."

That gets even Jackie to snicker, but Alain almost rolls off the bed, right onto the empty cupcake box. Which he then drops on my head. "That's for taking the mystery out of it."

"Not *all* MMO players have tiny penises," I point out. "Just most."

The episode ends, and Alain gets up to switch to the next DVD in the set so we don't have to let the title screen roll on. "Are you still planning on meeting with the executive type tomorrow?"

"I don't know," I answer honestly. "Harding said that Summers was trying to avoid the controversy. That means avoiding me."

"He can't avoid it anymore," Jackie says, and turns her laptop around to face the rest of us.

SummerStorm's official website and the Council of Gerents have appeared on the scene, like the goddamn Prince of Verona.

IT HAS COME to our attention that, outside the auspices of GeeKon, where a majority of SummerStorm's development staff is currently occupied addressing the needs of our consumer base, a riot masquerading as a so-called "guerilla panel" has been scheduled at a hotel near the convention center.

SummerStorm wishes to publicly and unequivocally condemn this display, and has asked that GeeKon staff revoke the badges of any convention attendees caught at the scene, with those who resist collection being barred from future GeeKons and any event at which SummerStorm has been invited to present.

The post has several thousand shares already.

"Ha-ha, Laura's going to need a bigger room," Alain says.

"Yeah," I agree, but correct, "*we* are."

CHAPTER TWENTY-THREE

Maybe it's the part of me that's lived in New York, but I keep searching out cops and find none. The hotel across the street from the convention center looks like the con *en miniature*, complete with a line around the door, but no one's collecting badges and no one's getting arrested. At least not yet.

And here I thought we Musketqueers would be okay arriving an hour early. People already have their phones out, snapchatting the line for its sheer length. Or in their hands, waiting to document the inevitable drama. *The Annals of #GuerillaPanel*, maybe. I know that half of these people are just here to say they were here, and maybe ten percent are trolls, and that any meaningful discourse is almost certainly going to get heckled down because there's no ban-hammer in the real world. But still. Anyone who's here, for whatever reason, is proving us right for getting the room in the first place.

This might be the only time in my life that there's been no such thing as bad press.

Jackie forbids me from tracking the hashtag or going online at all. I'm inclined to agree with her because I *will* lose my nerve if I do, no matter how confident I think I am. Alain keeps me distracted in line by messing with my outfit. I still have on one belt too many by the time we get through the door.

Apparently $3,000 nets a pretty big ballroom. It's got folding chairs wall-to-wall, and people are sitting double and clearly don't give two shits about the legal occupancy. With no con staff here to make people conform to some semblance of an orderly queue, people are clustered everywhere, especially around the front, phones and cameras at the ready. There are still some seats left, but not three in a row, so Jackie decides she'll sit in the back so she can type, and Alain and I go sit together. Toward the middle of the back, behind what looks like the entire Iwatobi swim club and one power ranger. Alain takes my hand and doesn't let it go.

The ballroom supposedly fits seven hundred, seated. With no room at all remaining, there could be as many as fifteen hundred people in here. It feels like even more.

Hotel security frames the doors, and lo, there *is* a police officer. But he just stands there, arms crossed like a bouncer. It's gross, but strangely fitting, that I have to wonder whose side he's on. Alain holds my hand tighter.

Up on the dais, Laura and the other panelists finish setting up. I didn't text her, since I knew she had so much to deal with, but now I wish I had. She looks ecstatic, brimming with nervous energy—she looks like I feel on an opening night. The other two, Jahata and a small Asian Vancouverite of indeterminate gender, seem just as in awe as she is, and Orin just looks like hell warmed over. Then the screen boots up, and a deafening cheer fills the ballroom and then some.

"How many are still outside?" Laura asks into the microphone, presumably of the security at the door.

One of the suits peeks out, followed by the cop, and then the suit turns back. "Too many," he shouts.

"Then leave the door open," Laura says, "and let's get started."

I don't think the applause is going to die down anytime soon. There are some boos mixed in, and a couple of catcalls, but they're mostly drowned out in the cheering.

"Before we even introduce ourselves," Laura begins, "I want to say that yes, you can tape this panel. You can tape us talking, or you can tape people in the audience responding to us, or both. If anyone isn't okay with the possibility of turning up on camera, you're welcome to leave. I can't promise a safe space, but I *do* promise a vigilant one. I am a law student, Jahata and her girlfriend Lexi are both licensed associated press, and Officer Guttierez is wearing a chest camera. If anyone says or does anything in here that can be considered illegal, it will be documented, and it will be considered court-admissible evidence. Hate speech is illegal in Washington State. Threats of violence are illegal in this entire country. And anything you say in this room will have thousands of witnesses. Furthermore, in the interest of full disclosure, Officer Guttierez is not the only member of the state police in attendance, so if you think you can take one for the team and have him escort you out so that someone else can commit a crime, you're dead wrong."

If I hadn't already wanted to throw myself at her feet, I would now. By the sound of the room, I'm not the only one. But some people *are* trying to leave, a few skulking, others hurrying out. Whatever their reasons, they're making room for more, and the traffic at the doors is so thick I can't see through it.

But I shouldn't be looking, Laura's speaking again.

"Now that that's over with, let's get started. As most of you know, this panel was originally affiliated with GeeKon, but cut at the last minute. We aren't affiliated with the convention at all, and I'd like to thank everyone who made it possible for us to secure this room. We raised a little more than we needed to, and the overflow is going to Stat Boost's client charity The Developer's Room, which provides elementary school kids with educational games and workshops. Stat Boost is also recording this panel as a podcast—hey Dan, what's up?—so we're live! And any ad revenue is going straight to The Developer's Room too.

"So without further ado, welcome to Diversity in Gaming! Let's go down the line and introduce ourselves."

Orin clears his throat. "Hey," he starts, "I'm Orin from Aqueabilitas—"

"So much for diversity!" someone shouts from the crowd. "Why's there a cishet white dude on the panel, huh?"

I wish I could say there isn't an uproar, but at least it's a small one. Orin waves his hand to try to calm them down. "I'm not white," he clarifies, "I'm Jewish. And I'm not heterosexual." I swear he looks straight at Alain—well, not straight. Ha. And Alain snickers and shakes his head, but I definitely catch a smile. "Guilty as charged on cisgender, though. But I'm not here because of my diversity credentials. I'm here because I was recently doxxed on behalf of my connection to Duchess Fatiguee and the *Eternal Reign* drama these last few months. I'll admit that I'm new to thinking about diversity in games as a political issue instead of an academic one, and that I might not be up here if I hadn't experienced this abuse firsthand."

He turns to Jahata, who is next to him, and yields the mic to her. Then Bobby takes their turn, and Laura hers, and we're back where we started. There are still some hecklers, but they get respectful clarifications from everyone on the panel.

"So," Laura proclaims once that's done, "the reason we formed this particular panel, and why it's gone in this direction, is because of a contest held by SummerStorm's MMO, *Eternal Reign*. It was publicly announced that a player, going by Duchess Fatiguee, won that contest. She was almost immediately dogpiled by other *ER* players."

"Allegedly!" someone yells.

"She made it up!"

"Just an excuse to quit!"

"Pics or it didn't happen!"

"And why isn't she speaking for herself?" That one came from the row behind me.

"Yeah! Why'd she send a man to fight her battles?"

"Fatiguee didn't send me," Orin snaps into the microphone, loud enough that it cracks. "I'm speaking on my own behalf. As some of you are so fond of saying, abuse doesn't only happen to women. I'm speaking about my own experience. It's different from what Fatiguee endured, but it's still real. I'm not fighting her battles. I'm fighting mine."

"'Cause she's a coward!" That same person behind me is apparently having a field day with this. Alain squeezes my hand. "If she can't take the heat, she should get the fuck out!"

"I did," I shout. "It didn't work."

Somewhere, in the pixilated land of Altestis, there's a scene similar to this one: the gerents have come together to deliberate Fatiguee's fate, regardless of her presence. And then she speaks up. It's the stuff of *Spartacus* and *Huckleberry Finn* and *Notting Hill* and *Much Ado About Nothing*: one voice from the crowd heralding a change in fortune. And even if the people here aren't in their finest armor, they're all wearing the trappings of geekdom and flying their colors proudly, and so should I.

I stand up. Laura catches my eyes and keeps them, and I nod. "*Bonjour*," I tell the world. "*Je suis Fatiguée* of all this bullshit."

To say that pandemonium ensues would be a gross understatement. I'm not the only one out of my chair. I'm not the only one staring at the dais. I'm at the center of a nexus of smartphone cameras and applause and invective, but I don't say a word after that. I just stand here, and keep my eyes on Laura's, and wait.

Being here is a fight. Standing is a fight. But this one I can win. I've won it, as long as I stay in the game.

"Everyone," Laura's voice cuts through the crowd, "I give you the Duchess Fatiguee's player."

Alain gives me a nudge, out toward the aisle. Up on the dais, Laura extends her hand. I didn't expect this, but I can accept it, and I edge out of the row of folding chairs. People part for me on the way up to the stage; some swoop closer, phones and cameras out, trying to get my face. At least one person lunges for me but someone else holds him back—and I think I recognize Ivan up front out the corner of my eye, but I keep walking. It already feels *better*, having said what I said. Coming clean. Not safer, but better. Liberating.

In the very front row, right at the foot of the stage, all four of the East vs. West panelists have seats. Krozin's here too, seemingly ready for a fight. And yes, there's Ivan, looking for all the world like I hit him in the nuts with a baseball bat. I get up on stage and don't smile.

Orin gets up from his chair so I can sit in it. I nod politely but wave him off, and he sits back down. I take his microphone and stay in front of the panelist table.

It's so different than being on stage: without the brights in my face, I can see the entire audience, and I know just where they're looking. And I can guess what they see—

—but I won't. What They See doesn't matter.

What I Say does.

"Yes," I begin, English a little shaky but good enough to continue. "I played Fatiguee. And I compiled the *Annals of Altestis* that won the contest. I have screencaps dating back to the exact hour of the announcement of my victory that show the campaign of harassment I experienced before Orin went public about it. The harassment coincided with a coup by several of my counts. I think there's someone else here who can set that record straight, if he doesn't mind being put on the spot."

Even before I catch Krozin's eyes, he's stood up in the front row. He projects well, without a microphone, "I didn't start it."

"Horseshit," Orin mutters, and I turn to wave him off.

I glare down at Krozin, right into his face. "I believe you. Come up here and say that."

He accepts the challenge with a sneer and a nod, and comes up to the microphone. I hand mine to him; behind us, one of the others disconnects theirs and passes it across to me. It feels like a rap battle for a second, not that either Krozin or I would make sense at one, but hey.

"Fatiguee was running what we call a court game," Krozin explains, "like Diplomacy or model UN—or Risk, actually. I'd been planning the coup for over a year and wanting to take Altestis for longer. Fatiguee set it up that she'd be absent for periods of time, sometimes months, and she'd appoint regents in the interim based on who was bringing her the most tribute. It was meant to push the bounds of gameplay, because she was basically letting us create our own missions and run our own levels. So I built a power base and bided my time, and when Fatiguee showed up after two weeks of absence—unannounced—I started the coup. I had no idea why she'd left."

Laura asks, behind us, "You're saying you didn't know that people were flooding her inbox?"

"Correct. I invited new players to support the coup, but that had been going on for months, before the contest winner was announced. It was a sleeper cell, not a Zerg Rush. Either Fatiguee or Sachem—sorry, Orin—approved them all."

Before Orin can say anything, I speak up. "That's the part that gets me. The day of the coup, you had almost thirty new Knights for me to approve—"

"Because you didn't authorize Sachem before you fucked off, like you usually do," Krozin cuts in. "I knew something was up, but you can't fault me for taking advantage of your error. That's the kind of game we were playing. That's how *Eternal Reign* works. If you can't duck in under your opponent's guard, that's a missed opportunity."

"No, it's *chivalry*," Orin says.

"It's neither." I shake my head. "It's a choice. Both are legal. Orin, you're right that if Krozin knew *why* I'd left without announcing it, it would be unethical for him to take advantage of it. But Krozin's right that I screwed up. And taking advantage of the fact that I screwed up was *cheap* and rude, but that's how he plays the game."

I expect Krozin to look smug when some people applaud, but he doesn't. Just level and cool. "That's how we all play the game."

"No. That's where you're wrong." I turn to him and steel myself to say it. "Not everyone is playing by the same rules you are. If they were, they wouldn't have flooded my inbox. And you invited those players in, thinking they were after the same thing as you. They weren't."

"And what do you want me to do? Tell them what they can and can't do?" He hisses through his teeth, glares up from the microphone. "That game is *built* on players doing whatever they want. I can't lure them in with the promise of an open world and then box them up."

"Yes, you can," Laura says. "I do. But it's not boxing them up: think of it like speed limits. They work by consensus. People disobey them all the time, when no one can see. And if everyone disobeys them together, that's a new consensus. But there's still a point where one person is driving too fast, and that's when the danger starts."

"Try telling that to people who've played GTA and F-Zero their whole life," Krozin jokes.

"Thank you, Krozin, for the best metaphor for privilege I have *ever* heard." Laura grins, and the room bursts into laughter and groans. She tips her hat at the crowd and turns her smile on me. "Would you have knowingly let people into your domain if you thought they were going to target players, not characters?"

"Never," I answer. "And, Krozin, I understand feeling like you can't stop them. But I don't understand feeling like you shouldn't."

"No one should," Ivan projects from the front row. "If they can shit-talk me, they can shit-talk you. And their right to insult me is the same as my right to insult them."

"When does it stop being insults? At what point does an insult turn into a threat?" Orin asks behind us. It's probably rhetorical, knowing Orin, but he waits long enough for someone else to answer. Maybe he really is learning.

"I think it has to do with the concentration of insults," Laura says. "If it really were just one person, and just one word, in an otherwise decent space, maybe someone could let it slide. But when it's all you see when you log on, that's a hostile environment—and I think you and I can agree that throwing a brick through someone's window is more than an insult."

Ivan goes sheet white.

Laura's smile fades, but her eyes are still shining behind her glasses. "It was him, right, Jahata? Lexi?"

Down in the press seats, Lexi checks her digital camera, smirking. But Ivan doesn't give her a chance to answer, just lunges out of his seat, already trying to pry the camera out of her hands from ten feet away. Oh, how the tables have turned: this time, there are so many more people to hold him back. And police to drag him out.

Since it's impossible to carry on with the panel while someone's possibly getting arrested—something I never thought I'd say—I half sit on the table and catch my breath. Orin offers me a glass of water, silently. I take it. And thank him.

Krozin's still onstage, staring after Ivan as he's escorted out with an expression that screams *derision*, eyes narrow and hard. "Idiot," he mutters, just loud enough for me to hear.

"I completely agree." I don't quite smile at him either, but I do nod politely and cover up the microphone. "I believe you about the coup, but I don't think you were completely ignorant. Not with your job."

"No, I wasn't," he admits. "But that was after the fact. And for what it's worth, I'm sorry. I never wanted to win on a technicality."

His last words to me in-game flash through my ears: *"I hoped you'd put up more of a fight."*

"You won the match," I say. "But I'm still in the game." And *now* I smile, and he smiles back.

He extends a hand to me—his left, since the right is holding the microphone. "I await your challenge."

I take his hand and give it a firm shake, then look over my shoulder. "Are you up for it, Orin?"

"Always," he says. "My la—my *liege*." He blushes a little. On the one hand I want to roll my eyes at that, but on the other, he's trying. The best I can do is meet him halfway.

By now, Ivan's out the door, and Lexi with him to present the camera as evidence. Laura calls the panel to order again. "All right, everyone. Now that we've got one less problem, how about we do something constructive?"

I already thrived on applause. I've never quite received it for this reason before, but I could get used to this.

Laura clears a space for me, next to her. I take it.

I guess even cumulonimbus clouds have silver linings: the panel runs for two solid hours, which would have been very much against GeeKon rules. Honestly it feels more like a summit in its own right than a con meeting. Now that the more personal drama is over and done, the discussion centers itself on methods of instating diversity from the top down, or at least from the middle out. Laura shares her findings on community cultivation, and Orin has some ideas about weeding the ignorant from the toxic. People come into the aisles and share their ideas and experiences, and one person in the audience has a job offer from Stat Boost by the time we're ready to wrap up.

I'm probably going to have to listen to the podcast later, to get the details. I'm still on that high, that *weightlessness* of coming clean. Of having my story understood and accepted, not just by those with stories like it, but by some from the supposed other side. Frankly, the issue's too multifaceted for there to be sides. Experience works in four dimensions, not three.

I take Laura's hand under the table, and she pulses hers around mine, a signal. *I get it. I'm there too.*

It's going to take time to clear the room, and even after we say we're ready to wrap up, people crowd the dais with questions for all of us, so the audience doesn't so much disperse as reconstitute. The middle of the room thins out, but now there's an enormous throng of people trying to leave and a fairly large cluster right in front of us.

Which means none of us on the dais sees the shouting for what it truly is.

"You can't do this!"

"Fuck off!"

"Let us out!"

And then a rather distinctive voice cuts past it on a megaphone.

"You will all turn in your badges," Harding says, somehow smug through the distortion. "None of you are permitted reentry to the con center. Comply or face arrest."

Laura scrambles to turn her microphone back on. "Don't listen to him! He's not affiliated with GeeKon. He works for SummerStorm!"

"You can believe me or you can believe her, but either way, I'm taking your badges. This panel isn't sanctioned and you are here illegally."

"We rented the room with our own money and we aren't on convention grounds!"

"Then you're not attending the convention, and you won't attend next year either." The crowd surges, and I clearly hear Harding laugh into the megaphone, once, brusque and dismissive. "Go ahead. Have your little revolution. We'll see how many of you get arrested."

"Mal, what in the sam hill is going on?" someone yells with a voice like Brian Blessed, booming all caps through the crowd. "Wasn't I supposed to have a meeting with that contest winner? Why isn't it in the con hotel? And why weren't any of *you* at my panel?"

Not two hours ago, this very room went silent for my confession. I never thought I'd hear, or rather, *not* hear, that silence again.

But for me, it was longer than a moment, or at least it felt that way. This time, it only takes one person recognizing Martin Summers, president of SummerStorm Entertainment Inc., for the room to burst into squeals and awe.

CHAPTER TWENTY-FOUR

Lunch is on Summers.
Lunch is on Summers.

Lunch, presumably for five, is on Martin Summers, president of SummerStorm Entertainment Inc., and if that weren't awkwardly surreal enough, I'm sitting at a hotel steakhouse table beside him, and he's already ordered a pint of something local and indicates that I should too. And Laura. And Orin. And when the waiter gets to Harding, who's looking about as frothy as the beer, Summers waves the waiter off and tells Harding to hold on a minute.

"You're still on the clock, Mal," Summers says. "At least until I get through another story. It looks like you kids've got quite the annals out-of-game as well. What should I call you, IRL?"

I tell him Daphnis, right from the start, and then it occurs to me: he probably knew my name from my file. They have my license, and I'm still Daphne on paper. But he still asked what I want to be called. And he asks the same of everyone at the table, which takes long enough that the waiter returns with four beers and five glasses of water, which he sets down in turn while Harding shifts uncomfortably in his seat.

Summers is broad and rounded, like a political cartoon from the twenties, with skin almost as dark as Laura's but no freckles and close-cropped hair that's gray at the temples and black everywhere else. And he listens patiently while we all trade off telling the story of the last few weeks, complete with the email exchange on my phone.

"'The intern responsible has since been fired,'" Summers quotes, incredulous, and turns a level glare on Harding. "And here I was, wondering why the Veeps kept linking me to Reddit."

"You can't prove anything," Harding mutters into his water glass.

"I don't have to." Summers hands me back my phone. "Clearly I need better publicity."

It takes a long moment of silence for the rest of us to figure out what he's saying.

"So how about it?" he asks me, in particular. "You want his job?"

Harding sputters.

I gape for a few seconds, then manage, "Sorry. I'm not sure how comfortable I feel about that right now. Ask again in five years, when you've fired a few more people."

Summers grins ear to ear. "Well, I'll start with this one. Mal?"

Harding chokes out a strangely dry "Yes?"

"Game Over."

At least Harding looks like he knew it was coming. He stands up, tips his hat, then offers Summers a handshake, and Summers leaves him hanging. The stink-eye Harding gives me could curdle milk, but I just glare back until he turns off in a huff, nearly toppling the waiter.

Summers sighs. "I promise, he wasn't this much of a tool when I hired him."

"I find that hard to believe," I admit, and Laura snickers into her beer.

"I mean it," Summers says. "I never imagined he'd use company resources to pursue a vendetta. I've probably got to screen the rest of my staff too. Who knows how he got hold of those chat logs? And that photo?"

"It might not have been him," Laura says. "That's the trouble with this whole situation. Even if he started it, it's more than he could have done alone."

Orin shakes his head. "He could only have gotten them from someone who got them from my computer. Those chat logs were on my old laptop at my parents' house on Long Island. The ones that weren't public, I mean. He couldn't have gotten them; he was three thousand miles away. The police are already looking into it—"

Summers sets down his pint. "Son, how long have the *police* been involved?"

"Since the doxxing cost me my teaching job."

Orin fills Summers in on *that* side of the story, and Summers immediately flags the waiter over to order another round of drinks.

"And all this because you won the Novelization Contest." Summers looks down into his beer, grits his teeth. "Because of my game."

Laura shakes her head. "Because of how other people played it. Or because you created an environment, not a game, and the only way these trolls knew how to play was to cut other players down. About the only thing you could have done was take us seriously sooner. And not doing that? That *is* your fault."

"I know it takes time," I cut in, because insulting the person who's already bought us two drinks each can go too far. "And I know that we've all been told it's easier to just ignore the trolls until they go away. But it's not. Once it happens, it happens, and even walking away is still a reaction. So if you're going to react, you have to react decisively."

"Well, here's a decision." Summers smiles and drums his fingers on the glass. "On my end, I keep hearing that paid mods would cost us too much money and wouldn't be in the spirit of the game. Based on this, I have to disagree with the board. I'll push through the Report Abuse measures and make sure there's a paid gerent on every server to deal with disputes. Sound good so far?"

It's a start, I think. "If you can come through on it."

He nods. "As for your drama, we were already going to make your *Annals* part of the over-story. I think elevating Fatiguee to a vicegerent once she reclaims her realm would be a step in the correct direction."

That would wrap her story up much better than a tragedy in a hotel room. She'd be an NPC like Doctor Conesto, but hey, there are other games. "It's a start," I agree.

"Right, right, it's only in-game. As for out here . . . are you sure you don't want Mal's job?"

"Very. I'm not qualified."

"Well, what are you qualified for?"

I grin. "You read the *Annals*. I think I'm qualified to rule a moderate-to-large fief."

The four of us laugh for so long that the waiter comes over and asks if we're okay.

Yes. Yes, we are. Or I am, at least.

In theater, the day we break down the set is called Strike. It's usually a huge celebration; a time to kick doors out of their frames and sing other people's songs and spread the last dregs of the cast in-jokes in the hopes they'll catch on.

Watching the convention break down is eerily similar. Laura and I stroll through the con center holding hands while the placards fold up and the ugliness of the bus-seat-cover carpet is revealed and the dealer's room turns back into a concrete wasteland. And for all the stress and fatigue surrounding us, people are still laughing. Hopeful. They've had tribulations this weekend too—definitely not the same as mine, but maybe one of those gofers was in the room next to ours and heard the brick come through our window, or that Deadpool-Vader hybrid was at the guerilla panel—and so they have stories. Someone's going to write up this con. Laura already has.

She squeezes my hand, like she feels what I'm thinking. I send a pulse back.

"So," she says. "That happened."

I bang my head on her shoulder laughing. Yes. That's all this weekend was: it happened. The understatement of the multiverse, and yet so true. She wraps her arms around me, and I can feel her laughter too, like mine's contagious. I hold tight.

We both know how to pull back without letting go. Our foreheads touch, then the tips of our noses, and her glasses are maybe a little in the way but that hasn't stopped us kissing yet—

And my pocket buzzes with Billy Flynn singing about all the shit he doesn't care about, except love. Right against Laura's leg.

"Let me guess," she grins, "your agent?"

I can't fight down the blush, and don't bother fighting the grimace. "First time he's cockblocked me, sorry." I sigh and untangle myself enough from Laura to get at my phone. "*Bonjour*, Julio."

"English, Daphnis," he says, "and wow is it refreshing to be called by my choice of name on the first try. "Are you still on the West Coast?"

"Yeah, until tomorrow. Any reason?"

"Only that I've got you short-listed for a dance-double role if you can get to LA in the next 24 hours."

I don't drop the phone, but it's a near thing. "*What?*"

"B-budget indie project, Sundance director. Details in your email. I need to know now because they're breathing down my neck: can you stay?"

"Um. One second." I try not to flail at Laura too much. "Do you know anyone in LA who can put me up for a night? Or, shit, anyone who can drive me there?"

I will never get enough of Laura's smile. It just climbs up her cheeks all the way to her glasses, and then she bites her lip, and it ties me in the *good* knots. "Bet your ass I do. If you're up for a road trip with me and a night on Gramma's couch."

I nod, maybe a little too quickly, and tell Julio on the phone, "I can stay. But if I have to fly back, you're paying."

"Ha-ha. Then you'd better not have to fly back. Knock 'em dead, kid. Oh—one more thing: I already warned them about your headshots not matching up yet. Send me a quick no-filter of the haircut for now, and I'll pass it along. They know who to expect."

The rest of the call goes pretty quickly, but those words stick with me: *they know who to expect.* They reverberate in my head all through the good-byes and good-lucks, and through Laura squealing and whirling me around.

"Tell me everything in the car!" she cheers, already tugging me down the hall. "And call Jackie and Alain to meet you with your stuff. We don't have much time if you need to be in LA tomorrow."

Something hasn't quite hit me. "You're sure?"

Rather than answer, she kisses me. Hard. Right here in the con center lobby. Holding my hands (and the phone) behind my back just how I like it, so I know she's boss.

Yeah. Yeah, we're both sure.

 EPILOGUE

At the close of a seven-hour siege, Fatiguee, an armada behind her, places her hand on Duke Krozin's forehead. He is cowed before her, spent of all his weapons and wiles. His allies are scattered, his henchmen lost to the fathomless deep.

"Here we are again, Krozin," Fatiguee says, the air redolent about her with ozone and craft. "Have you enjoyed your rule, brief as it was?"

"Immensely," he snarls, unrepentant to the last.

Fatiguee smirks, eyes narrow and cold. "I brought you a souvenier," she says, and beckons Sachem to her side. Her dearest of counts holds in his hands a reliquary, and he brandishes it before Krozin, his eyes as bright and unforgiving as the crystal.

Krozin visibly balks. "You didn't."

"I did," Fatiguee corrects, "and you'll be pleased to know I intend to enshrine it. I literally own your soul, Krozin. Feel free to tell what remains of your fleet. I'm sure it will amuse them to hang this over your head. Now get out of my keep. If you can."

[Text] [Voice] [Video]

Video should be fine for this, and once the window boots up, there's Neal.

"Well fought," he says, and as far as I can tell he's being genuine.

So am I. "You too."

"Is this going in the *Annals* too?"

"That's up to the story team, but I think so. Do you mind?"

He shakes his head. "As long as I've left my mark. I need to concentrate on my new series anyway. Tell Summers he needs some new material."

"He already knows," I say. "But I'll remind him."

"Take care."

"You too."

I can't tell who closes the window first, but it doesn't really matter, and there's not much else to do in game either, so I close that out too. The gerents will take care of the rest. I'll check in with them at work tomorrow: I can swing by the story offices on my break from motion capture. I never thought that I'd be acting for animators, but it's a pretty awesome gig, and I've already got contracts with other companies in Seattle and LA so I'm not completely tied to SummerStorm.

Laura drapes herself over the back of my computer chair, nuzzles my neck. "Resolved?"

"As it's going to get." I tilt to kiss her, but mostly just get her glasses pressing into my cheek. So I correct that error of choreography and kiss her properly, which ends up with *both* of us in the chair, but I'm not complaining.

At least not until my phone buzzes. With a FaceTime request from Alain.

That's right, it's midnight back on the East Coast. It's so easy to forget that there's a timezone difference between me and the other Musketqueers now. I'll probably get used to it eventually, but I might never get used to not being with them. "We have to take this," I groan, and Laura lets me up just enough to get the phone and prop it up so both of them can see both of us.

Alain waves, and Jackie pokes her head in. "*Bonsoir*, lovebirds!"

"It's good to see your face," I half sing, and Laura, who gets the joke, bursts out laughing.

"Did the last of your boxes arrive?" Jackie asks.

"Not yet. UPS says tomorrow."

"We packed a few surprises in there," Alain says. "You'll know when you see them."

"Alain—"

Jackie cuts me off. "They're not for you, they're for D'Artagnan."

It takes me a second, but it doesn't take Laura that long. "I'm honored," she says, bowing a little. "I promise to uphold the ideals of the order."

"You'd better." Alain taps the screen accusatorily. "And if you don't, you'll have to face all three of us."

This is getting embarrassing. "How goes the roommate hunt?"

Alain sighs. "You'll never guess who just applied."

"They don't have to," Jackie says. "It's Orin."

I blink. "He didn't mention it to me."

"He probably didn't want to get your hopes up." Alain rolls his eyes. "Since we may well turn him down."

Jackie clarifies, "You have right of first refusal. If you don't want him in this apartment, we won't take him."

I shake my head. "If it's fine with you both, it's fine with me. He's still my friend. But you have my permission to toss him out on his ass if he pisses you off."

"Done," Alain says, and Jackie nods. "All for one," he starts, and now four voices chorus, "And one for all!"

Dear Reader,

Thank you for reading Erica Kudisch's *Don't Feed the Trolls*!

We know your time is precious and you have many, many entertainment options, so it means a lot that you've chosen to spend your time reading. We really hope you enjoyed it.

We'd be honored if you'd consider posting a review—good or bad—on sites like **Amazon, Barnes & Noble, Kobo, Goodreads, Twitter, Facebook, Tumblr,** and your blog or website. We'd also be honored if you told your friends and family about this book. Word of mouth is a book's lifeblood!

For more information on upcoming releases, author interviews, blog tours, contests, giveaways, and more, please sign up for our weekly, spam-free newsletter and visit us around the web:

Newsletter: tinyurl.com/RiptideSignup
Twitter: twitter.com/RiptideBooks
Facebook: facebook.com/RiptidePublishing
Goodreads: tinyurl.com/RiptideOnGoodreads
Tumblr: riptidepublishing.tumblr.com

Thank you so much for Reading the Rainbow!

RiptidePublishing.com

ACKNOWLEDGMENTS

So many people have made this story happen, and not enough of *their* stories resolve nearly so well.

Before I even get to my friends and colleagues, I want to acknowledge Felicia Day, Mikki Kendall, Anita Sarkeesian, Zoë Quinn, Brianna Wu, and countless other people who have experienced cyber-mobbing and doxing. This book isn't just *for* you, it *owes* you, and so do I. The magnitude of what I've experienced online isn't nearly at the levels you've survived (and I hope it never will be), and your bravery and forthrightness inspire me every day. This story is my way of keeping your issues out there in an increasingly dismissive and oversaturated world, and lending my own voice to the discussion.

Caz is an amazing editrix and sounding-board for my myriad and perpetual anxieties; Sarah is an indestructible lioness; Alex is a hardass but I adore them anyway and am super thankful for all their exacting effort; and LC makes everything pretty. Bobby Ng belongs to Heidi Belleau and appears at GeeKon courtesy of Rear Entrance Video.

Now to bring the accolades closer to home: instead of tackling this tale on the MTA like I ordinarily would (because seriously, what the fuck is going on with the NYC subway this year), I wrote practically all of this on Ray's couch, and edited it on Chuck and Bec's. For the first time, I kvetched on Twitter with Chasia, Cass, Kelly, and James throughout the process, which was more helpful than I ever guessed it could be. Pucik hooked me up with his old friends from EVE Online, which was a huge inspiration and a great help. And I always wrote with Aria, Gil, Eric, Racheline, the Emilies both Tall and Dead, and especially Hilary in mind, and their occasionally inebriated wisdom in my ear. Between them, and my increasingly bewildered but mostly supportive family, I was never far from someone who wanted this book to hit the shelves.

And Abbi. Who I was never far from at all. Who I love with all my heart. Because my amazing wife is going to change the world like she changed mine: for good.

ALSO BY
ERICA KUDISCH

About the Author

Erica Kudisch lives, writes, sings, and often trips over things in New York City. When not in pursuit of about five different creative vocations, none of which pay her nearly enough, you can usually find her pontificating about dead gay video games, glueing rhinestones to her face, and making her beleaguered characters wait forty thousand words before they get in the sack.

In addition to publishing novellas and short stories as fantastika-focused alter-ego Kaye Chazan, Erica composes under her given name and is responsible for the BDSM musical *Dogboy & Justine*, and serves as creative director and cofounder of Treble Entendre Productions.

She also has issues with authority. And curses too fucking much.

Twitter: @EricaKudisch

Instagram: instagram.com/hardhandmaiden

Enjoy more stories like
Don't Feed the Trolls
at RiptidePublishing.com!

Looking for Group
ISBN: 978-1-62649-446-6

Player vs Player
ISBN: 978-1-62649-184-7

Earn Bonus Bucks!
Earn 1 Bonus Buck for each dollar you spend. Find out how at
RiptidePublishing.com/news/bonus-bucks.

Win Free Ebooks for a Year!
Pre-order coming soon titles directly through our site and you'll
receive one entry into a drawing for a chance to win free books for
a year! Get the details at RiptidePublishing.com/contests.